A SHOT IN THE DARK

Rolfe Wade decided that Slocum was going to spend the rest of the night in bed with Monica, and he thought that he sure couldn't blame him for that. He said good night to the boys in Applegate's and staggered out the door. Part of it was drunkenness, and part of it was the gimpy leg that Slocum had given him.

He found his horse at the hitching rail and climbed on before turning it west and riding slowly out of town. Down at the west end of the street, the town was dark. It would be darker once he got out on the road, but that didn't bother him.

Then he saw the figure raise a shotgun and point the barrel in his direction. He recognized the man, but it was too late, for there was the blast, and it blew Rolfe Wade clear back out of the saddle. He landed hard in the dirt with a dull thud, his chest a torn-up mess of red.

His thoughts and his breathing had both stopped for good . . .

JAKE LOGAN

SHOWDOWN AT DROWNDING CREEK

JOVE BOOKS, NEW YORK

SHOWDOWN AT DROWNDING CREEK

A Jove Book / published by arrangement with
the author

PRINTING HISTORY
Jove edition / January 1996

ISBN: 0-515-11782-X

A JOVE BOOK®
Jove Books are published by The Berkley Publishing Group,
200 Madison Avenue, New York, New York 10016.
JOVE and the "J" design are trademarks
belonging to Jove Publications, Inc.

PRINTED IN THE UNITED STATES OF AMERICA

10 9 8 7 6 5 4 3 2 1

1

John Slocum measured off six yards of calico, picked up the scissors and cut the yardage off the bolt. He put down the scissors and replaced the bolt on the rack. Then he folded the calico cloth and laid it aside.

"Anything else for you, Miz Tilton?" he asked.

"Well, I'm not just sure yet," said the dumpy, middle-aged woman. "Why don't you just put that over on the counter while I look around some?"

"Yes ma'am," said Slocum, and he took the calico and walked back around the counter, tossing it down next to the cash register. The lady stopped by a fashion book and was slowly turning the pages.

Just what the hell am I doing here? Slocum asked himself. Then he recalled that he had come into Drownding Creek just a little over a month ago, dead tired, flat broke, hungry enough to eat raw lizards, and wearing an empty Colt at his side. When Matthew Crocker had offered him a job clerking at his general store, he had agreed without even asking about the pay.

He remembered telling himself that he was getting too old for the wandering life, the ranch work, fighting work, driving stagecoaches and freight wagons, and all the things he had done for so many years, which had taken their toll on his old bones and muscles. He was tired of dodging fists and bullets. He was tired of empty pockets and missing meals. He was tired and sore from sleeping on the ground too many nights. He was tired of being outside in bone-chilling cold and in driving rain, and by God, he was just plumb tired.

A good, steady, indoor job had been just what he needed, he had told himself. He would never get rich working for old Crocker, but if he watched his money and didn't drink, gamble, or whore too much of it away, he would never miss a meal again, and he would never sleep outside on the hard, cold ground in a rainstorm again. The job didn't pay much, but the pay was regular, and it offered a room in the back of the store where he could sleep.

He reminded himself of all these advantages of his job and of the miserable shape he had been in when he had taken the job—jumped at it—as he watched Mrs. Tilton pick cans off the shelf, read their labels, and put them back. *Busybody*, he thought. *Old bitch*. He wondered if she and her husband did anything in bed besides listen to each other snore.

Maybe, he told himself. *Maybe years ago when they were younger*. Then he recalled the several

times he had come close to getting himself hitched—
or at least had allowed the thought to enter his
mind—and he told himself how lucky he was that he
had never allowed himself to get snared in that way.

Why, it was just possible that old lady Tilton had
been a real looker when she was younger, and old
Tilton had thought that he had just bought himself a
ticket to heaven on his wedding day. Slocum wondered where Tilton thought that ticket had finally
taken him.

Mrs. Tilton came over to the counter and put down
a jar of Heinz plum preserves, a can of Blanke's Mo-
jav Coffee, and a couple of pocket-sized bags of Gen-
uine Durham Smoking Tobacco, the kind with
papers for rolling your own smokes.

"For my husband," she said. "I wish he'd give it
up, but he's just stuck with the craving, I guess. Are
you a smoking man, Mr. Slocum?"

"I like a good cigar every now and then," said Slocum.

"I see. Well, if you'll just write all this down, my
Henry will be around later to pay the bill."

"Yes ma'am," said Slocum. He was entering the
purchases and the amounts in the book when the bell
over the door tinkled. He glanced up to see Rolfe
Wade come in.

"Give me a plug of that Union Leader," Wade said.

"Be with you in a minute," said Slocum.

He finished Mrs. Tilton's tally and turned the book
around for her to sign. Then he wrapped her purchases carefully, taking his time just to annoy Wade,
and handed her the package.

"Thank you," he said. "Come back again."

"I will," she said. "Good day, Mr. Slocum."

Wade stepped up to the counter.

"Do I get that plug now?" he said impatiently.

Slocum gritted his teeth, turned around, and picked a plug out of the Union Leader box. He turned back toward Wade and tossed it on the counter. He'd had about as much of this life as he could stand. He remembered his condition when he had ridden into town, and he remembered all the reasons he'd had for taking the job. Still, he'd had it, right up to his nose.

"Mister," he said, "a decent man waits his turn, especially when a lady's in front of him."

"Hell," said Wade, "all I want is just that damn plug. You was writing all that shit down, and then you had to wrap that old biddy's stuff up. You could have tossed me the plug and I could have tossed you a dime and been out of here before you was done writing. Wouldn't have hurt you or the old woman none. Besides, you're slow as the mail."

Wade reached for the plug, but Slocum scooped it back up off the counter before Wade's hand could touch it. He turned and put it back in the box. Wade slapped a dime on the counter.

"Give me that damn plug," he said.

"You don't like the way I do things here," said Slocum, "take your business somewhere else."

"There's my dime," said Wade. "Give me the plug."

Slocum knew he was being stupid. If Crocker caught him treating a customer like this, he'd fire him on the spot, but just then, Slocum didn't give a shit. He was thinking that if Crocker did not fire him, he'd just quit this damned job anyhow. He'd been wearing an apron for too damn long as it was.

He picked up the dime, reached across the

counter, and dropped it into Wade's shirt pocket. Yes, he told himself, he was being stupid. Wade's jaws tightened in anger. And Wade was a big man and probably just half Slocum's age.

"I told you what you can do with your business," said Slocum. "You want me to tell you what you can do with your dime?"

"Slocum, is it?" said Wade.

"Yeah. Slocum."

"Well, Slocum," said Wade. "I reckon old Crocker might not realize what an asshole son of a bitch he's got working in his store. So I ain't holding it against him, and I ain't aiming to mess up his place here. So let's you and me just step outside into the street and get it on. Right now."

"I can't do that, Mr. Wade," said Slocum. "You see, Mr. Crocker pays me to be right here inside this store until closing time. If I was to go outside with you, while I was busy stomping your face in the mud, someone might come in here and steal old Crocker blind."

"When's closing time?" said Wade.

"Six o'clock," said Slocum.

"I'll be waiting for you right outside."

Slocum smiled.

"That's just fine," he said. "I'll see you then."

Wade stomped out of the store and slammed the door behind him. Slocum turned around and got the plug back out of the Union Leader box. He took a dime out of his pocket and put it in the cash drawer, then stuck the plug in his pocket.

It was not a busy day. Ordinarily, Slocum would have found it unbearably boring, but his anticipated fight with Rolfe Wade had raised his spirits remarkably. He knew it was stupid, but that didn't matter a damn bit. He'd been living a lie for too long, and he was ready to break loose again. Wade had just come along at the right time, and Slocum was ready. It didn't really even matter, he told himself, if he wound up getting the shit stomped out of him. He'd feel better anyway, having made the right decision at last.

Slocum checked the clock on the wall. It was six. He reached under the counter for a key, walked to the front door, and locked it. Glancing out the window, he saw Rolfe Wade waiting in the street. He also noticed a crowd of men lined up on both sides of the street. Obviously, Wade had boasted around town what he was going to do to Slocum, and the crowd had gathered to watch the fight. Slocum grinned.

He turned around the sign that said Open on one side and Closed on the other, pulled down the shade, walked back behind the counter, and returned the key. Then he went back to his room. He figured he had just quit his job. He hadn't told Crocker yet was all. So he packed up all his belongings, rolled them in his blanket, and tied it up. He threw the roll over his shoulder and walked out the back door, locking it behind him. He pocketed the key. He'd give it to Crocker later, when he told him about his decision.

Slocum walked around the building and out onto the sidewalk. Just in front of Crocker's store, he tossed his roll down by the wall. Then he stepped up behind the line of men waiting there to see the fight. He put a hand on the shoulders of two men standing side by side.

"Excuse me," he said.

The two men turned and saw Slocum. They moved

quickly aside to let him through the line, and he stepped down into the street. Wade was looking in the other direction just then.

"Looking for me?" Slocum called out.

Wade turned.

"I was beginning to think you wouldn't show," he said.

"Boy," said Slocum, "I've ate better men than you for breakfast."

Wade lifted his fists and moved toward the center of the street. "Come on, old man," he said.

"Whip his ass, Rolfe," someone shouted from the crowd, and then the noise from the onlookers was both general and constant. Slocum stepped forward to meet Wade halfway.

"You tell anyone where to send the body?" said Wade, and then he swung a hard right, but it was wide. Slocum blocked it easily with his left, and drove his own right hard into Wade's belly. Wade made a whoofing sound as he felt the punch and backed off a couple of steps, but he still stood upright. His belly was hard.

Wade moved in again and swung another right, just about like the first one, and Slocum blocked it the same way, but this time Wade's left followed fast and it caught Slocum on the side of the head, staggering him. Slocum popped out a quick left jab in retaliation. It smashed Wade's nose, causing it to bleed.

"Damn you," said Wade, and he moved in, flailing with both arms. Slocum guarded his face with both his hands and ducked low, running hard into Wade's midsection and grabbing him around the waist. Then he stood up, lifted Wade high into the air, and tossed him back over his own head.

Wade yelled out as he felt himself flying through the air, but his yell stopped when he landed hard on his back. He lay there, trying to suck some air back into his lungs.

"Get up, Wade," someone shouted, and the rest of the crowd noise was a roar. Slocum shook his head to clear it, and he watched Wade there on the ground in front of him gasping for air. He knew the big man would be up soon, and he thought about kicking him a few times while he was down. He decided against that tactic, as good as it was, because of the partisan crowd. He waited.

Wade caught his breath and got himself to his feet. He looked at Slocum and raised his fists again.

"Come on, you bastard," he said.

Slocum stepped forward, jabbing with his left, and then somehow one of Wade's roundhouse rights caught him on the side of the head, and it felt like it jarred his brains loose. He staggered back a couple of steps, felt his knees buckle under him, and fell. Wade moved in quickly, kicking at Slocum's head. Slocum covered it with his arms, and Wade aimed his next kick at Slocum's ribs.

I should have done that when I had my chance, Slocum thought, as he rolled away from a kick. Then, while Wade was still off balance, his right foot still in the air from a kick, Slocum rolled toward Wade, rolling hard and fast against the left leg.

Wade shouted out in pain and fell over. Slocum got to his feet. Again he thought about kicking, but again he remembered the crowd. It might not matter to them that Wade had kicked first. He was their favorite. Slocum backed off and waited.

Wade got up, favoring the left leg. It wasn't broken, but it was hurt. He hobbled toward Slocum with hate written all over his face, but his hurt leg kept him off balance. Slocum popped his nose with a couple of jabs, then hit him with a hard right to the jaw that staggered him.

With Wade hurt and off balance, Slocum moved in fast to finish the job. He hit Wade with a left hook on the ear, then another hard right, and Wade dropped. He tried to sit up, but he couldn't make it. He looked up at Slocum and spoke, but the crowd was shouting so much that Slocum didn't hear what he said.

"What's that?" Slocum shouted.

"I can't go on," said Wade, raising his voice as much as he could. "I'm done."

2

Slocum stepped over to Wade and gave him a hand up, and Wade looked a bit puzzled as Slocum offered his right hand. Even so, Wade shook hands with Slocum.

"You whipped me fair," he said.

"You're a tougher nut to crack than I thought you'd be," said Slocum. "Can you walk on that leg?"

Wade staggered a couple of steps to test it.

"Yeah," he said. "I'm all right."

"I'll buy you a drink," Slocum said.

"Well, hell," said Wade. "I'll let you."

"I'll just get my gear," said Slocum. He walked over to the store and picked up his blanket roll from where he had tossed it. He slung it over his shoulder and walked back out into the street to join Wade.

Then the two of them together, bloody and bruised, headed for Applegate's Palace.

On the way, Slocum ducked into Rosie's, paid her fifty cents for the right to a bed in the large upstairs room for the night, and asked her to hold onto his bedroll until morning. He rejoined Wade on the sidewalk, and they hobbled together the rest of the distance to Applegate's. As they stumbled in through the swinging doors, a great cheer went up from the crowd gathered there. Most of them had been out on the street earlier to watch the fight. A cowboy bought them their first drink, and a traveling salesman bought their second.

"Hell, Slocum," said Wade, "I'll fight you every night of the week if they'll keep on treating us like this for it."

"I don't know how long I'd last," said Slocum, "but it would be a hell of a lot of fun along the way."

Slocum was beginning to feel just a little bit woozy, and he hadn't yet spent a dime out of his own pocket. He was starting to think that Wade's idea of a fight in the street every night wasn't such a bad one after all. Then he felt something soft press against his side, and a soft voice whispered in his ear.

"You want to go upstairs?"

Slocum turned his bleary eyes toward the voice, and he saw a big-eyed, tiny blond staring up at him. He blinked, trying to get his eyes to focus.

"With you?" he said.

"That's the general idea," she said.

"I'd sure like to, honey," said Slocum, "but I don't believe I've got the price."

"That's okay," she said, still whispering. "We'll

work something out. Just don't tell anyone. Come on with me. I like your style. I didn't think anyone around here could whip Rolfe Wade."

"You like a fighting man?" Slocum asked.

"Like I told you," she said, "I like your style. You coming?"

"You God damn right," said Slocum. "Just lead the way."

Wade saw them as they started to climb the steps to the rooms upstairs. He knew where they were going and what they were going for. He'd been up there more than a few times himself.

"Hey, Slocum," he yelled. "Watch out for that one. She's a hard bucker. She's liable to throw you clear off the bed."

"I know how to ride," said Slocum. "And I know how to fall."

They went the rest of the way up the stairs to the sounds of laughter and catcalls below.

"I bet you do, too," she said, as she led him to a door.

"Do what?" he asked.

"Know how to ride."

She opened the door and stepped inside, pulling Slocum after her by his arm. He shut the door behind himself as he stepped in. She led him to a chair and had him sit, and she took his shirt off. He watched her turn and reach toward a table nearby, and he heard the soothing sound of water as she poured it from a pitcher into a bowl. Then she was washing his face with a wet towel.

"Ouch," he said.

"Did I find a tender spot there?" she said, and she leaned over and kissed his forehead. He looked up, and she kissed his lips. She finished washing the blood and dirt off his face, and she washed his neck and arms and hands. His knuckles were skinned, and she kissed his hands.

She put the towel aside, and she knelt down in front of him. She pulled off his boots and socks, and then she looked up into his eyes. His vision had cleared some by then, and he was beginning to feel his blood stir. She reached up to unfasten his belt buckle and then his fly, and when she grabbed the waist of his trousers, he put a hand on each of the arms of the chair and heaved himself up enough so that she could pull them out from under his ass.

He sat in the chair stark naked, and she was still fully dressed. She put her hands on his knees, and she slid them slowly all the way up his thighs. His cock rose without even being touched, and she looked at it, wide-eyed, for a moment. Then she looked up into Slocum's eyes, and she smiled.

She moved her hands down to the insides of his thighs. One hand went beneath his balls and weighed them in its palm, and the fingers closed and squeezed them lightly. The lively cock jumped up, and she grabbed it with her other hand and squeezed it and held it hard. Slocum moaned and let his head fall back on the chair.

She inched closer on her knees, getting herself in between his legs, and then leaned forward. Suddenly her tongue shot out and flicked the head of his cock, and the cock throbbed, trying to buck and jump, but she still gripped it hard in her hand. She licked it again, this time in earnest, her tongue lapping its head, rolling around and around and under and over the cock head, and then, with no warning, she clamped her lips around it and sucked it hard. She took her hand away and slowly drew the whole length of the thick and throbbing cock deep into her warm, wet mouth. Slocum groaned out loud.

God, he thought, *such a tiny little girl with a tiny little pouty mouth. Where did she put all that cock?* At the same time, he humped his hips forward, trying to drive it in deeper, and he reached down with both hands and held her head.

She kept her lips locked tight around his thick cock as he rocked back and forth in the chair, holding her head, fucking her face. She still held his balls in one hand, and with the other hand, she reached under and behind the swollen sack to tickle him there with her nails, and the scratching almost drove him mad.

"Ahh," he moaned, and he humped faster and harder. He was afraid that he would bruise her lips or mash her nose, driving into her face like that, but he couldn't help himself. He couldn't stop. She was making him crazy. Scratching. Tickling. Holding the sucking pressure with her tight, tiny lips.

The pressure inside him was building up until he could hardly stand it, and he knew that he was ready to burst. He felt it build and pulse, and finally there was a mighty gush from his cock into her mouth, and then another and another. He moved forward in the chair, still holding her head tight against his crotch, as his thrusts became involuntary twitches and his once mighty gushes became spurts and finally a slow ooze.

With a long and heavy sigh, he eased his grip on her head, letting his hands slide down the sides of her face, and he settled back in the chair and relaxed.

She still sucked hard even as she backed off the cock, sliding it slowly out of her mouth, and then she squeezed it with a milking stroke and licked the last drop away. She stood up and looked at him, and started to unfasten her dress. Slocum looked up at her with lazy eyes.

"Say," he said.

"Yes?"

"What's your name?"

"Monica," she said. "You want to go to bed now?"

He watched her finish stripping, and he thought that she was as lovely a little thing as he had ever seen. She was small, but she was almost perfectly shaped: smooth, with soft curves in all the right places.

"Yes," he said.

She reached out to take him by the hand, and she pulled him over to the bed. He stood and watched as she tossed back the covers, then crawled in, her lovely ass pointed right at him. He crawled in after it.

Rolfe Wade decided that Slocum was going to spend the rest of the night in bed with Monica, and he thought that he sure couldn't blame him for that. But he was getting bored with the company in Applegate's, so he decided to leave. He'd look Slocum up sometime tomorrow maybe and ask him if he'd had a good night.

Wade decided that he liked Slocum after all. The man knew how to fight, and he didn't hold a grudge. Slocum wouldn't be the first friend Wade had made for himself by fighting with him first. Hell, he thought, it was the best way there was to get to know a man real fast.

He said good night to the boys in Applegate's and staggered out the door. Part of it was drunkenness, and part of it was the gimpy leg that Slocum had given him. He thought that he'd go on over to Rusty's for a few more, but then he almost fell off the sidewalk once he got outside, and he realized that he was farther gone than he had thought. He decided then that he would just go on home.

He found his horse at the hitching rail and climbed on board with some difficulty. Then he turned it west and started to ride slowly out of town. Down at the west end of the street, the town was dark. It would be even darker once he got out on the road, but that didn't bother him. Hell, he told himself, he could pass clear out in the saddle, and that old horse would just take him right straight on back to the ranch.

He passed the windmill and was riding along in front of the livery stable and feed store, the last building on the west edge of town, when a figure stepped out of the shadows from behind the far corner of the building. Wade raised his head a little and squinted his eyes. Something didn't seem quite right to him, but his head was reeling, and he wasn't thinking very clearly. *Son of a bitch*, he thought, *I'm drunk as hell*.

He saw the figure raise a shotgun and point the barrel in his direction, and then he recognized the man, but it was too late, for at that moment there was the blast, and it blew Rolfe Wade clear back out of the saddle. He landed hard in the dirt with a dull thud, his chest a torn-up mess of red. His thoughts and his breathing both had stopped for good. The man with the shotgun vanished.

Slocum heard the shotgun blast, but he didn't think anything of it. Drunken men were always shooting something off in the night. Besides, he had more important things on his mind than anonymous gunshots somewhere out in the darkness.

He rolled on his side facing Monica, and he put a hand on a breast and squeezed it gently. Then he rolled on top of her and kissed her lips, as she moved her legs apart to let him in. He was on his knees, and she reached down with both hands to grip his cock and balls, and he could feel the life coming back into it.

"Oh," she said. "I think you're ready to go again."

His cock throbbed in her grip, and he knew that he was ready. He moved his hips down, and she pulled the cock toward her waiting cunt. When he was close enough, she rubbed the head of the cock up and down between the lips of her luscious pussy, and now it was her turn to groan.

"Oh, John," she said. "Give it to me."

He drove it in hard and deep and the force of his pelvis slamming against hers jarred her whole body, but she reached around him and gripped the cheeks of his ass in her hands and pulled him toward her, at the same time driving her own hips upward.

"Ah," she cried. "Ah, God. Fuck me, John. Fuck me, you son of a bitch. Fuck me hard."

He started to thrust and hump and drive with everything he had, and underneath him, Monica slammed her hips up to meet his downward plunge. Their bodies came together with a slap. They pounded themselves together until they were both sweating and almost worn out from the effort, and then together they slowed down.

His movements became slow and gentle, and she responded in kind, and their lips met and parted, and they dueled with their tongues. She spread her legs wide apart and lifted them, then wrapped them around his waist and held him tight that way.

"That's good," she said.

Slocum pulled back until his cock almost slipped out of its sheath, and then he drove it in again all the way.

"Oh," she said, "do that again."

"Don't worry," he said. "I think I might could keep this up all night."

And he just about did.

3

She was already gone when he woke up naked and alone in bed. He wondered if she had gotten a call to service another customer, a real paying customer maybe. Well, hell, he couldn't worry about that. She had given him one hell of a night, and he was grateful for that.

But he had other things to think about, more important things, like the fact that he had just fought himself out of a job. He had not yet seen old Crocker since well before he had braced Wade in the store. He could just ride on out of town without ever saying a word, but he thought that he owed Crocker better than that. After all, Crocker had given him a job and a place to sleep when he was dead broke and sure as hell needed them both.

He decided that he would wander back over to Rosie's, where he had paid for a bed that he had never used, and pick up his blanket roll. Then he'd go to the livery stable and retrieve his horse. He had enough cash on him to do that. He'd saddle up and strap the blanket roll on and be ready to ride out. Then he'd look up Crocker and tell him that he quit.

Crocker owed him a little money, and he would collect that. At least he wouldn't be riding out of town broke, the way he had come in. He also still had the key to the back door, the door that went into the room he had been staying in. He had to return that to Crocker. But mainly, Crocker needed to know that Slocum would no longer be keeping the store for him. He would either have to find someone else or do it himself.

Rosie's downstairs was an eatery, called Rosie's Fine Food. Upstairs was one big room with several beds. Slocum had already stopped by for his blanket roll, so he was walking into Rosie's for the second time that morning, but he felt better this time. He felt better than he had felt since he had hit town, for he was no longer pretending to be something or someone other than himself.

Just outside, his big Appaloosa was saddled and waiting, and Slocum was again wearing his Colt, rather than a God damned storekeeper's apron. He looked around at the customers already eating in Rosie's, hoping to spot Crocker, but he didn't see the man anywhere.

It was almost time to open the store, and he thought that he really should go look up Crocker before he did anything else, but he was hungry as hell, and after bailing out his horse, he had just about enough left in his pockets for a good breakfast. So he found an unoccupied table and sat down.

Jill Hooley, the girl who served the customers, set the tables, washed the dishes, and even made the beds and emptied the chamber pots from upstairs, came right over.

"Howdy," she said. "What can I get for you this morning?"

"Coffee," said Slocum. "Hot and black. And a regular breakfast."

Rosie's regular breakfast consisted of three fried eggs, a mess of pan fried potatoes, several thick slices of bacon, all sliding around on a greasy plate, and a couple of big, fluffy biscuits and a bowl of brown gravy on the side. When Jill brought the coffee, she smiled and said, "I seen your big fight last night."

"I reckon most everyone in town saw it," said Slocum.

"I'd say so," said Jill. "You done real good."

"I got in a lucky punch or two," said Slocum. He caught himself looking Jill over real carefully, and he realized that she must have been aware of his looks, and she must have known what he was thinking about.

She was young and lovely. She wore a dirty apron, and she was sweating from the hot work, and he could see that the shirt she wore under the apron was clinging to her breasts because of the perspiration. Her brown hair had been fixed up nicely, but here and there errant strands strayed away and dangled out of place.

He tore his eyes away, picked up his coffee, and

took a sip. It almost burned his tongue. He was getting ready to leave town, and he didn't need to be thinking about another tumble. Besides, all she had given him was a friendly smile and a comment about a fight. That wasn't enough to indicate an interest in anything further.

"It looked like it was more than just luck to me," she said. "Well, I'll be back with your breakfast in just a few minutes."

Slocum was sopping up the last of his gravy with a piece of biscuit. Jill had just refilled his coffee cup. He thought that he sure hated to leave town just as that ripe young thing had maybe shown an interest in him, but he had made up his mind. It was time to move on. And he still had to find Crocker to tell him he had quit, get his money, and give back the key.

Just then he heard the unmistakable sound of the hammer on a single action revolver being pulled back to full cock just behind his head.

"Don't move a muscle," someone said. "I'd hate to blow your brains out all over that table. It'd spoil everyone's breakfast."

Slocum sat still.

"Not to mention mine," said Slocum. "Who are you? And what's your beef with me?"

He couldn't think of any enemies he'd made during his short stay in Drownding Creek, other than Rolfe Wade just last night, and Wade had certainly given him the impression that he held no grudges.

"It's Sheriff Bryce," said the voice. "And I've got a deputy on each side of me. That's three guns, so don't try anything stupid."

"Well, I ain't too bright," said Slocum, "but I ain't

about to try anything with three guns on my back. What's this all about?"

"Charlie," said Bryce, "get his gun."

Out of the corner of his eye, Slocum could see the deputy called Charlie move up close and reach for the Colt. He could feel it as Charlie slipped the Colt out of his holster. *Damn*, he thought, *I should have just left town as soon as I got my horse. That's what I get for worrying about the feelings of other folks.*

"Now, stand up real slow," said Bryce.

Slocum scooted the chair back and stood, holding his arms out to his sides.

"You got money on you to pay for this meal?" asked the sheriff.

"I wouldn't have ordered it if I didn't have," said Slocum. "You ain't arresting me for trying to cadge a meal, are you?"

"Just dig it out and lay it on the table," said Bryce. "Move slow."

Slocum did as he was told.

"Now, pick up that coffee cup in your right hand," said Bryce, "and bring it along with you to the jailhouse."

Slocum picked up the coffee cup. It was so full that a little slopped over the edge.

"I've got some change coming," he said.

"Leave it for a tip," said Bryce. "Now get to walking."

"Where are we going?" Slocum asked.

"Like I told you," Bryce said. "Straight to the jailhouse."

Slocum walked slowly and carefully, his eyes on the full cup of hot coffee in his right hand. When they reached the jail and got inside, Bryce stopped Slocum in front of the big desk. He ordered him to put down the cup and empty out his pockets onto the desktop. Then he had him take off the gun belt.

"Now get your cup and move on over there into that cell," the sheriff said.

As the iron door clanked shut behind him, Slocum turned to face Bryce and the two deputies for the first time.

"I'm about as helpless as I can be now," he said, "so will you tell me just what the hell this rousting is all about?"

"I'm sure you know," said Bryce. "It's about Rolfe Wade."

"You mean this is all over that fight I had last night with Wade?"

"I reckon you could say that," said Bryce. "In a way." He hung the big key ring back on the hook on the wall and sat down at his desk around the corner from the cell where Slocum stood and out of Slocum's view.

"You arrest people for fistfighting in this town?" Slocum yelled. "Well, hell. Why don't you have old Wade in here with me then? I know I whipped him, but I'll bet he didn't press no charges against me for it. Shit. We even had a few drinks together after the fight. Over at Applegate's."

Charlie stepped over to the cell door and snarled through the bars at Slocum. Slocum thought that the deputy looked like an angry rat.

"You know damn well that Rolfe didn't press no charges, don't you?" Charlie said.

"What do you mean?"

"You know, 'cause you killed him last night."

"What?"

"Shut up, Charlie," said Bryce. "Go on and have your breakfast. You and George both. Go on, now."

He waited until the two deputies had left the office and shut the door behind them. Then he got up and walked over to the cell.

"Slocum," he said, "someone shot Rolfe Wade last night as he was riding out of town. Blasted his chest away with a shotgun. Maybe you done it and maybe not, but you're the only suspect I got right now, and I mean to hold you till I get the whole thing figured out."

"You think I killed him because of that fight?" said Slocum. "Hell, sheriff, I won the fight."

"The point is," said Bryce, "you did fight with him. Just now I don't know of anyone else who was even mad at him."

"You said someone shot him last night," said Slocum.

"That's right."

"The last time I saw Wade he was standing at the bar in Applegate's, and I was on my way up the stairs with Monica. I didn't get out of that bed until just a short while before you slipped up on me this morning."

"I don't know how much good a whore's word will do you," said Bryce, "but I'll check your story out with her just the same."

Bryce walked back to his desk and sat down again.

"Well," said Slocum, "are you going to talk to Monica or just sit around here?"

"I said I'd talk to her."

"When?"

"When I damn well get around to it," said Bryce. "You just sit down and keep your mouth shut. I'll let you know what I find out when I'm good and ready."

"That's easy for you to say," said Slocum. "You got me locked up in here for something I didn't do, and you won't even check out my story. Hell, I was fixing to leave town. I got my horse all saddled and packed and—"

"I know all about that," said Bryce. "And you know what, Slocum? That don't look too good for you either, under the circumstances. You fixing to run off like that the morning after Wade got killed."

4

Sheriff Harlan Bryce walked into Applegate's Palace and found Monica sitting at a table near the bar. She looked like she had sure enough had a rough night, and he wondered why she was even up so early in the day. He stopped at the bar and ordered a cup of coffee for himself, took the cup to the table, and sat down directly across from Monica.

"Morning," he said.

Monica smiled a crooked smile and looked across the table through bleary eyes at Bryce.

"You're not looking for some this early in the morning, are you sheriff?" she asked.

"Hell," he said. "I got my own. I don't have to come here for that."

"A little change every now and then might do you

some good," said Monica. "You and her. Hell, lots of men come to me to save their marriages. You know?"

"There ain't nothing wrong with my marriage," said Bryce, "and I didn't come here for cunt."

"Oh. You want a piece of ass then? I'm game."

"I came here to ask you about last night."

Bryce sipped his coffee.

"What about it?"

"Did you, uh, entertain John Slocum last night?"

"What do you care?" she said. "You one of them that likes to hear it told about? Well, honey, that Slocum's a hell of a man. You can take it from me. Is that what you wanted to know about him?"

"Slocum says he was in your bed all night last night," the sheriff said. "I need to know if he's telling the truth. That's all."

Monica suddenly became serious.

"Is he in some kind of trouble?" she asked.

"I've got him in jail," said Bryce. "He's under arrest for suspicion of murder. Someone gunned down Rolfe Wade late last night."

"Oh, no," said Monica. "Rolfe? God. Why? He liked a good fight, but—God. Well, anyhow, it couldn't have been John Slocum. Me and him went upstairs together and left Rolfe standing down here at the bar. You've got the wrong man in jail, Harlan baby."

"What time was that?"

"What?"

"When you went upstairs with Slocum. What time was it?"

"Hell, I don't know what time it was. I just know that we went upstairs together and Rolfe Wade was down here. That's all I know."

"Did you stay with Slocum upstairs?"

"That's the general idea, ain't it? I don't just tuck them in bed and say nighty night."

"Were you up there with Slocum all night?"

"Well—"

"All night?"

"I left him sometime, two, three in the morning. I don't know. He was stark naked and sound asleep, and he had a big smile on his face."

"Thank you, Monica," said Bryce. He turned in his chair to face the bar. "Frank," he said.

"Yes sir?" said the bartender.

"What time did Wade leave out of here last night?"

"I couldn't really say, sheriff," said Frank. "It was pretty busy in here last night. He was here pretty late. That's all I can say for sure. When it gets that busy, I can't keep track of their comings and goings."

"After Slocum went upstairs with Monica here," said Bryce, "did you see him come back down?"

"I never," said Frank.

"Course there's always the back door," said Bryce, more to himself than to either Frank or Monica. He picked up his cup and drained it of coffee, then stood. "I guess that's all," he said. "Thank you both."

"That's the way it is, Slocum," Bryce said. "You got no alibi. We don't know what time Wade left Applegate's, and we don't know what time he got shot. We don't know what time Monica left you sleeping in her bed, neither. From all we know, you could have done it. And you're still the only one I know of who had a reason."

"That's crazy," said Slocum. "I didn't have a reason. A fistfight ain't a reason to kill a man. Especially when I won the fight, and we went and had drinks together afterward."

"I reckon we'll just have to let a jury decide that," said Bryce.

"You mean you're actually going to charge me with that killing?"

"I'm thinking about it real hard," said Bryce. "Yeah. I think I probably will."

"You son of a bitch," said Slocum.

"Careful," said Bryce. "You don't want to show too much of that temper. You look to me like you'd like to kill me right now."

"I probably would," said Slocum, "but that don't mean I killed Wade last night. God damn it to hell, anyway."

Slocum lay on the dank and smelly mattress on the jail cell cot pondering the situation he was in. He told himself that he should never have stopped off in Drownding Creek in the first place. And having stopped off, he should never have taken a job and stayed around. But then, once he had the job, he opined, he should have forced himself to swallow his pride and remembered old Crocker's admonition, "The customer is always right." He should never have allowed himself to get into that fight with Wade.

But then, once he had gotten himself into the fight and there was no backing out, once he had whipped Wade, he should have just ridden on out of town. Or at the very least, he should have hurried out this morning. What a hell of a series of mistakes he had made, he thought. *What a damn fool I am. Pride and pussy have been my downfall.*

He decided that it was doing no good to think back and tell himself what he should or should not have done. He was in jail, and it looked very much like he was about to be charged with murder. He should be thinking of ways to get himself out of this mess.

He had tried telling the truth, and that had not worked. He couldn't think of a lie that would work, either. He thought about breaking out of the jail and hightailing it for the border. He had been a fugitive before, and he could live with it again. The life of a fugitive wasn't the greatest in the world, but it was better than the life of a jailbird.

But the cell was tight, and he had no friends outside who could be counted on to help him out. He could stay alert and watch for an opportunity to catch the sheriff or one of the deputies off guard, but beyond that incredibly vague plan of action, he could think of no other.

What else then? What else? If he couldn't pin down the time of the killing or the time Monica had left him alone, what other line of reasoning might there be? The sheriff had said that he had arrested Slocum because he couldn't think of anyone else who had a reason for wanting to kill Wade.

Well, by God, Slocum thought, *someone else had killed Wade, so someone else had to have had a reason.* Might there be some way of finding out who that someone else might be? Not sitting alone and locked up in a damned jail cell, there wasn't. That was for sure.

. . .

Billy Hooley rode up to the hitching rail outside of Rosie's and dismounted. He slapped the reins of his horse around the rail and walked boldly into the café. It was between mealtimes, and Jill was busy wiping down and resetting tables. Billy strode across the room to her.

"Billy," she said, looking up. "What are you doing here?"

"I want you to come home," he said. "Won't you?"

"I told you I won't," she said. "Not until Papa apologizes to me for the way he treated me and promises to change his ways."

"Papa's stubborn, Jill," said Billy. "You know that. I think he's sorry for what he done, but I know he won't ever say so. Come on home. He won't do it again."

"Billy, I'm twenty-one years old, a growed woman, and I can legally make my own decisions. I won't have him or anyone else slapping me because I went to a dance with a man, whether he likes the man or not."

"I don't blame you for that," said Billy, "but it just hurts me to see you working here like this. Papa won't hit you again. Come on home. Please."

"No," she said. "I can't. I won't."

"Papa would never have hit you if he hadn't been so worried about other things lately," said Billy.

"Maybe and maybe not. I'm sorry for his troubles, but I meant what I said. Go on now. I'm all right."

Billy heaved an exasperated sigh and turned to leave the café. He was almost to the door when Jill spoke again.

"Billy," she said. "Wait a minute."

He turned back to face her.

"What?" he said.

"Billy, did you hear about Rolfe Wade?"

"I ain't heard nothing," he said. "I just rode into town."

"He was killed last night. Shotgunned out on the street."

"Who did it?"

"The sheriff's arrested John Slocum."

"Slocum? The guy that works for old Crocker?"

"Yeah," she said, "but I don't believe that Slocum did it. Bryce arrested him 'cause Slocum and Wade had a fight out in the street last night, and Slocum can't prove where he was when Wade got shot. Bryce says that he can't think of anyone else with a reason for killing Wade."

"Boy," said Billy, "I damn sure can, but I don't think I could convince old Bryce."

Jill looked around to make sure that no one was anywhere near to listen. She found no one. Even so, she leaned in close to her brother and spoke low.

"If we was to find a way to break him out of there," she said, "you reckon he'd help us out?"

"I don't know," said Billy. "I don't even know him. Hell, he'd probably just get the hell out of the country as fast as he could. It'd be the smartest thing he could do. If he was out."

"You care if I have a talk with him?"

"About what?"

"About helping us. If we can get him out."

"First of all," said Billy, "how you going to get a chance to talk to him? Second, if you can talk to him, how the hell are we going to get him out of jail?"

"Let's just take one thing at a time," she said. "You care if I talk to him?"

"And if we get him out, what makes you think he'd stay around?"

"One thing at a time," she said. "Do you care?"

"Hell," he said, "I don't give a damn. Mostly because I don't think you can find a way to do it, anyhow."

"Billy, I want to help solve Papa's problems as bad as you do, and I'll tell you what. You stick with me on this deal, and we get Slocum out of jail, I'll quit this job."

"You mean it?"

"I mean it."

"All right," said Billy. "I'm with you. What do you want me to do?"

"Nothing right now. Just check back with me about this time tomorrow. Okay?"

"I'll be here," he said, and he left the café with mixed feelings. He wanted to get his sister out of there, but he wondered just what in hell she was about to get him into.

Slocum spent a long day in the jail cell, but it was an even longer night. He considered the irony of his situation compared to the previous night, and he went over in his mind the details of the delights of the time spent with Monica. If only she had stayed with him the entire night, then he would have a solid alibi for the time of the killing.

Then he caught himself. He was doing it again. Thinking about what might have been. It was a waste of time, and he knew it, but then, he thought, he sure as hell did have a lot of time to waste.

The remembrance of the night with Monica led him to dreaming of Jill from Rosie's place and all of the things that he would like to do with her if he ever got the chance. But he knew that if he ever got the chance to get out of this damned jail, he would keep going and never look back, not at Jill or Monica or anyone or anything. Just get the hell as far away from this damn place as fast as possible. And the only memory he wanted to hold of Drownding Creek was just enough of it to keep him from ever coming back. Well, maybe some memory of the night with Monica.

He did not forget his resolve to stay alert and look for a chance to escape, and he was well aware of his surroundings. He was the only prisoner in the small jail. There were three cells, and he was locked in the middle one. From his cell, Slocum could see the front door of the office that opened out onto the street, but he could not see the sheriff or anyone else who might be sitting at the sheriff's desk.

The building was shaped like an L. The shortest wing contained the office and one cell, and the other two cells were in the longer part, which shot off toward the alley. The sheriff's desk was against the back wall of the office and therefore around the corner from Slocum's cell.

Slocum was aware, though, that Bryce had gone home, leaving the deputy called George to sit at the desk overnight. Slocum had called out to George once, asking for a cup of water, and George had obliged him, but the deputy had been very cautious in passing the water to Slocum. He had not been wearing a gun, and he did not have the keys to the cells with him.

Even if Slocum had managed to grab hold of George, it would have done him no good. He couldn't have done anything but strangle him to death. Then, in the morning, the sheriff would have found George's body just outside the cell and Slocum still inside. There would be no question about that murder. So Slocum hadn't tried anything.

He had learned something. He had learned that he would have to come up with something a little more complicated than getting a drink or a meal and trying to grab the person who delivered it, in order to break out of this jail.

He had a window in his cell that looked out onto a narrow passageway that ran between the jail and the livery stable next door. There was nothing to look at but a wall, and the bars in the window were planted deep and solid. He had tested them.

He had no more ideas. There didn't seem to be any hope, but Slocum refused to give up. He had no intention of swinging for a murder he didn't do. The nearest thing he had to a plan was to just wait and watch. Someone might slip up and open his cell door, giving him a chance to make a break for freedom.

Short of that, there would be the trial. If he hadn't gotten himself out of this mess by then, they would have to shuttle him back and forth to the courthouse. He might find his chance there.

It was late when Slocum at last fell asleep on the lumpy cot, and his dreams were strange that night, ranging from replays of the night before with Monica; scenes in which he was being led up to a scaffold, having the noose placed around his neck and the trap door sprung, only to wake up in a sweat while still falling; to imaginary lovemaking with Jill.

He even dreamed once of blasting his way out of jail, a Colt in each hand, blowing numerous holes in Bryce, both of his deputies, and several onlookers. It was not a restful night.

5

"Good morning, sheriff," said Jill, as she shoved the door shut with her rear end. Her hands were both occupied with the large, covered tray.

"Howdy, Jill. What've you got there?"

"Breakfast for Slocum."

"I didn't send for no breakfast, Jill."

"I know, sheriff, but he overpaid yesterday morning, and I just figured that under the circumstances, he'd appreciate a good breakfast."

"Why all the concern, Jill?" said Bryce. "You ain't sweet on that drifter, are you?"

"If I was," said Jill, "it wouldn't be none of your business, but I ain't. It just happens that I don't believe he's guilty. That's all. You want to take a look at this tray so I can give it to him?"

Bryce stood up and walked around his desk. He lifted the cloth to examine the breakfast, then dropped the cover back down.

"Looks okay to me," he said. "You want me to take it in to him?"

"No. I can handle it. Okay?"

Bryce shrugged.

"Go ahead," he said. "I just don't see why you want to bother."

Jill walked around the corner and stopped at the door to Slocum's cell. Slocum stood up and walked over to look at her through the bars.

"What's this?" he said.

"Your breakfast," she said. "You hungry?"

"I could eat a damn horse."

Jill slid the tray through the slot provided for the purpose, and Slocum took it from her. He turned to walk back to the cot, but Jill stopped him.

"Slocum," she said.

He turned back to face her, a look of curiosity on his face.

"I don't believe you shot Wade," she said.

"Thanks. The sheriff sure seems to believe it, though," he said.

She gave a jerk of her head to indicate that she wanted him to come closer, and so he did. When next she spoke, it was in a whisper.

"Me and my brother aim to get you out of here," she said. "Be ready."

Slocum wanted to ask her about a dozen questions, beginning with why the hell she and her brother should give a damn, but before he could even open his mouth, she was gone. He stood staring after her for a moment, then walked over to his cot and sat down.

He lifted the cloth off the tray and dropped it beside himself. The breakfast was the same as the one he had ordered the morning before, and he wolfed it down ravenously. Then he drank the coffee. He felt better. He felt like he could take on ten men—or even better, ten women.

But of course, locked in the damn cell, the feeling was wasted. He thought about what Jill had said. She and her brother intended to break him out of jail. Why the hell should they want to do that? He didn't even know them. He had seen Jill in Rosie's, of course, but that was all, and he wouldn't know her brother if he saw him. What was their interest in his troubles?

Jill had said that she didn't believe that Slocum was guilty of the killing, but that didn't seem to him enough to merit their interference in the matter, certainly not to the extent of taking part in a jail break.

There had to be something about the whole deal that involved them in some way. There had to be, it seemed to Slocum, some way in which his escape would be to to their benefit. What could it possibly matter to anyone in Drownding Creek, he asked himself, if he were to hang? What could it possibly matter if he were to escape?

The only other person he could think of who might have a reason to give a damn was the real killer. Suppose Jill's brother had shot poor old Wade. And then, suppose that by some miracle or other, Slocum were to stand trial and be proved innocent. That would mean that the sheriff would have to admit that he had to look elsewhere for the guilty party, and a renewed investigation just might lead to the killer.

But if Slocum were to escape, he would look more guilty, and the sheriff would not be likely to search for anyone else. Slocum could get clean away or he could be killed in the attempted escape, and it would not matter a damn bit to the killer. Either way, he'd be in the clear, and Slocum would be pegged as guilty as if he'd received a guilty verdict in a court of law.

So the little bitch was setting him up for the benefit of her brother. He could think of no other reason for the offer of help. The question now was what to do when they made their move. If he went along with them, he would be falling into their trap.

Should he just sit tight on the cot and refuse to budge when they made their play? Should he tell Bryce what Jill had said to him and let Bryce worry it through? He didn't like the thought of telling a lawman anything about anyone.

Besides, he had every intention of making a break for it on his own, and if he alerted Bryce to the possibility of an attempted break, even coming from outside, it would just make the sheriff and his deputies that much more cautious. No, he decided. He wouldn't say anything to Bryce.

That still left the problem of what to do when Jill and her brother made their move. The best solution he could think of was to make his own move before they showed up. Break out on his own and get the hell out of the country. Ride far and fast.

This left his original plan unchanged, except for one important fact. The intentions of Jill and her brother made his lone escape more urgent. He had to act before they did.

He took the tray and its cloth cover over to the door and put them on the floor, but he held the empty cup in his hand.

"Hey, Bryce," he called.

"What do you want?" Bryce answered.

"Is there a chance of getting some more coffee in here?"

When Bryce came around the corner with a coffeepot in his hand, Slocum saw right away that the lawman was not wearing his gun. It must have been a policy of his jailhouse never to approach an occupied cell wearing a gun. It was a damn good policy, of course. It would be a fairly easy matter, when offered a cup of coffee or water or whatever, to grab the lawman's arm and jerk him up against the bars. Then, if he was wearing a gun, it would be possible, worth a try, to get hold of it. Bryce knew all that and took the appropriate measures to avoid it.

Slocum held his empty cup through the bars and Bryce refilled it.

"Thanks," said Slocum.

"Hand me that tray, and I'll take it out of here," said Bryce.

Slocum bent and picked up the tray, then slid it back through the slot for Bryce to take.

"Say," said Slocum, as Bryce was walking away, "I left a saddled and packed horse out there on the street."

"He's back in the livery," said Bryce. "Unsaddled. I've got your blanket roll and saddlebags here in the office. You ain't got a thing on the outside to worry about, so you might as well just relax."

"After my trial, when I'm declared innocent," said

Slocum, "am I going to have to pay a bill at the livery to get my horse?"

Bryce turned back to face Slocum.

"Slocum," he said, "if a jury finds you innocent, which I doubt, I'll pay the bill on your horse. I'll even buy you a steak and apologize for holding you up. Then I'll smile and wave good-bye as you ride out of town."

"I just wanted to know," said Slocum. "That's all."

Bryce disappeared around the corner, and Slocum moved back over to the cot to sit. He sipped the coffee. Bryce's coffee wasn't as good as that Jill had brought in from Rosie's, but what the hell? It was coffee.

He hadn't gotten a chance to make a play on Bryce, but he managed to get some vital information. His horse and saddle were in the livery. The rest of his stuff was right here in the sheriff's office. Knowing that made it easier to plan the break. Or at least, to plan his moves immediately after the break. He would grab up his belongings in the office, hustle on over to the livery, which was just next door, throw his saddle on the big Appaloosa, and get the hell out of town.

The only part of the plan that was still unformulated was how to get himself on the other side of the cell door.

"Hey, Bryce," he called out.

"What the hell do you want now?"

"I don't suppose it ever occurred to you that I don't even own a shotgun."

"Crocker does," said Bryce. "And you had keys to the store."

"Did you look at them guns to see if one had been fired recently?"

"You had time to clean it."

"I did not."

"Save it for the trial, Slocum. Now, see if you can keep quiet for awhile."

Slocum sat on the edge of the cot, fighting back an urge to call Bryce every foul name he could think of. He sipped some coffee and tried to think of a sane way to break out of Bryce's jail. Then he heard the front door open and close again, and he strained to listen.

"Hello, Matt," Bryce said. "I figured you might be coming around. Here's the key to your back door."

"Thanks, Harlan," said Matthew Crocker. "Can I see him?"

"Sure," said Bryce. "Right around the corner."

Slocum got off the cot and moved to the barred door to meet Crocker.

"Mr. Crocker," he said, "I'm sure sorry to leave you in the lurch like this, but—"

"It looks to me like you had no choice," said Crocker.

"Well, sir," said Slocum, "it ain't exactly the way it looks. You see, even if I hadn't have got myself locked up like this, I was planning to quit on you when old Bryce pulled me in."

"Why, how come, John?" said Crocker. "Not enough pay?"

"No. It ain't that. It's just that I ain't cut out to be a storekeeper, I guess. I guess you heard about that fight I had with Rolfe Wade night before last. Well, it started over his attitude in the store. I figured you'd most likely fire me anyhow when you found out about it."

Crocker sighed.

"Well," he said, "I'm sorry to be losing you, and I hope that you get this mess all cleared up. I know what they've charged you with, John, and I don't believe you did it."

"Thanks for that, Mr. Crocker."

"I owe you some money," said Crocker, and he reached into a pocket.

"It won't do me no good in here," said Slocum. "Why don't you just hold it for me?"

Then he thought about his escape plans, and he quickly corrected himself.

"Or you could leave it with Bryce to put with my other things."

"All right," said Crocker. "I'll do that. Is there anything else I can do for you?"

"Not unless you can find out who killed old Rolfe Wade," said Slocum. "I guess there ain't."

"If I recall," said Crocker, "you like a good cigar."

"That's true," said Slocum.

Crocker reached into an inside coat pocket and drew out a handful of cigars, which he gave Slocum. Then he took a tin of matches from another pocket and passed that through the bars.

"Well," said Slocum, "other than a bottle of good whiskey or a wild woman, both of which I imagine would upset old Bryce out there, I reckon this is just about the best thing you could have brought for me under the circumstances. Thank you again."

Slocum put a cigar in his mouth, struck a match, and fired up.

"Ah," he said. "That's just fine."

"John," said Crocker, "I understand that you're in here because you fought with Wade and you don't have an alibi. Is that all that Bryce has on you?"

"That and the fact that I was fixing to ride out of town," said Slocum. "But, damn it, if I was heading out because I'd just killed a man, I'd have left a lot sooner. Oh, yeah. And Bryce says that he just can't think of anyone else who had any reason to kill old Wade. That's all."

"Well, don't give up hope," said Crocker. "I'll ask around a little myself. See if I can't find out something about who might've had it in for Wade."

"I ain't giving up hope, Mr. Crocker," said Slocum. "Hell. They're talking about hanging me. I don't just sit back and relax and wait for a thing like that to happen."

6

Nothing happened the next day, as far as Slocum could tell from inside the cell. He wasn't able to get anything out of Bryce or either of the two deputies regarding their investigation, and he was beginning to believe that there was no investigation. They were convinced that they had their man, and they weren't going to look any further.

Slocum felt like he was going to go crazy. He felt like a caged animal. There was nothing to do but eat at mealtime, sleep if he could manage it, and smoke the cigars that Crocker had given him. He tried to come up with plans for his escape, but it was just no good. There didn't seem to be any way of grabbing anyone through the bars that would do any good, and any attempt to claw through or bust through walls

47

or bars was an even sillier idea. Nothing else occurred to him.

That night, as he was trying unsuccessfully to sleep, it came to him that he was awful close to hanging. Slocum wasn't afraid of death. He had courted it too long and much too often for that. But if he had any choice, he would rather postpone it a little longer, and if he had no choice, if he was to die soon, he did not want to go at the end of a hangman's noose. He made up his mind that if no other opportunity afforded itself, when they led him out of the cell to hang, he would fight them and force them to shoot him down. If he could not escape with his life, he would at least do his damndest to cheat them out of their hanging.

It was late, and Charlie was at the desk alone, Bryce and George having gone home for the night. Slocum was lying on the cot, unable to sleep. He realized that the noise had been going on for some time, but he had only just become really aware of it. It had begun with just a slight scratching, but it had gotten louder and much more obvious, and it sounded to Slocum as if it was coming from just outside his window. A chunking noise, a thump followed by a scratching sound. An occasional bump against the wall.

Suddenly Charlie was in the hallway, a lantern in one hand and a six-shooter in the other. Keeping a safe distance away from the bars, he held the light up and squinted into the cell.

"What the hell's going on?" he said.

"Damned if I know," said Slocum, "but it's keeping me awake."

Charlie squinted into the cell a little more. There was nothing to be seen. Slocum was lying on the cot. The noise continued.

"By God, that's right outside," Charlie said. He hurried back around the corner, and Slocum heard the front door open and slam again as Charlie ran out.

The deputy stepped into the narrow passageway between the jail and the livery stable, still holding his light, and he saw a figure squatted down beneath the window to Slocum's cell. The person had a shovel and seemed to be trying to dig under the wall. Charlie aimed his revolver and cocked it. The person stopped digging but did not turn around to face Charlie.

"Hold it," said Charlie. "Just what the hell do you think you're doing? You trying to dig old Slocum out of there? That's pretty damn stupid, you know it? Ain't no way you could dig under there. You just got yourself caught for nothing. Stand up slow and turn around."

Another figure moved into the passageway behind Charlie.

"Stand up," said Charlie. "You want me to blow your head off sitting there? Come on. Get up and turn around."

The other figure stepped up close behind Charlie and raised a hand, which held a club about three feet long. He brought the club down hard. There was a swish and a sickening thud, and Charlie's whole body went limp all at once. His knees buckled and he slumped to a sitting position, then fell over on his side. Billy Hooley tossed the club aside and picked up Charlie's revolver.

Jill turned away from the wall, grabbed up the lantern, and blew out the flame.

"Come on," said Billy.

They hurried around the corner and into the office. Billy stood just inside the door, watching through the window in case anyone should come along. Jill ran to the key ring hanging on a peg on the wall, then hurried around the corner to Slocum's cell. As she fumbled with the keys, Slocum jumped up off the cot.

Jill got the door unlocked and swung it open, and Slocum forgot all about the reasons he had for not going along with Jill's scheme.

"Let's go," she said.

Slocum paused at the sheriff's desk to look for his belongings.

"Hurry," said Jill.

"I've got some stuff here that I don't want to leave," said Slocum.

"We're trying to save your life here," said Jill. "Leave it behind."

"Go on ahead," said Slocum. "I can take it from here."

He found his gun belt, the Colt still in the holster, and he strapped it around his waist. In a desk drawer, he found an envelope with his name written on the outside. He stuffed that inside his shirt. His blanket roll and saddlebags, along with the Winchester in the saddle boot, were lying on the floor against the wall, and he picked them up. He looked up to see Jill and Billy still waiting beside the door.

"All right," he said. "I've got it all."

Billy took a quick look outside and saw an empty

street. He jerked the door open and stepped out, followed close by Jill and Slocum. Slocum turned to his left.

"Hey," said Jill. "Where are you going?"

"I'm going after my horse," said Slocum.

"We got him," said Jill. "Come on."

Slocum hesitated, wondering if he should believe this woman. He didn't want to leave town without the big Appaloosa, and he didn't want Jill and her brother, if that's who it was, to lead him into a trap. The saddlebags and blanket roll were in his left arm. He held the Winchester in his right. Quickly he cranked a shell into the chamber, just in case.

"Where?" he said.

"Right around there on the other side of the jail," said Jill. "Come on now."

Slocum followed her around the corner, and sure enough, three saddled horses stood waiting. One of them was his. They mounted up and started riding slowly down the back street out of town. Slocum's impulse was to turn his horse and run, to get the hell away from everyone and everything about Drownding Creek.

If he did that, he knew there would be a posse after him soon, and it would be a hard run to the border, and a toss-up whether or not he would make it.

These two were up to something. They had some kind of a plan, and likely it involved ducking any posse that might come after them. He argued himself into following along. Partly, he was just curious. He wanted to know why the hell they had bothered with him. Breaking a man out of jail could be a dangerous business, and if they got caught, it could mean a stiff charge. They had taken a hell of a chance. They had to have a powerful good reason.

Safely out of town, Billy picked up the pace a little. Slocum followed along and kept quiet for another couple of miles. Then he hauled back on the reins, stopping his horse.

"Hold up a minute," he said.

"We got to keep going," said Billy.

"How much farther?" Slocum demanded.

Billy shrugged. "Another eight miles," he said.

Slocum dismounted.

"Then I've got to get this stuff tied on properly," he said. "If I hold it much longer, my damn arm'll fall off."

"Well, hurry up," said Jill.

Slocum tied the blanket roll and the saddlebags in place. He strapped the saddle boot onto the left side, then stuffed the Winchester down inside it. He leaned against the saddle and looked up at Jill and at Billy.

"I want to know where you're taking me and why," he said.

"We'll tell you later," said Jill. "There's no time to waste right now."

Slocum turned and looked back over their trail.

"I don't see no one dogging our heels," he said, "and I ain't going no farther with you until I know what the hell's going on."

"All right," said Jill. "We're headed for an old line shack on our father's ranch. It's up in the hills yonder, and you've got a clear view for miles around from there. We've got it stocked up with supplies. It's a good hideout."

"I don't want a hideout," said Slocum. "I want to get out."

"And be a fugitive for the rest of your life?" said Jill.

"It's better than hanging," said Slocum.

"Best would be to prove you didn't do the killing," said Billy.

"Well," said Slocum, "I don't see no way of doing that."

"We might," said Billy.

"Why?"

"Look," said Jill. "Let's just say that it has nothing to do with you. We want to find out who really killed Wade for our own reasons. We thought if we busted you out, you might help us. That's all. Will you come on now?"

"I'll ride on with you for now," said Slocum, "and we can talk some more. If I don't like your story or your plan, I ride out."

"That's fair enough," said Jill. "Let's go then."

Slocum wasn't ready to admit it out loud to Billy and Jill Hooley, but the cabin was cozy, a hell of a lot nicer than the jail cell, and he was glad to be out and more or less free. Jill put on a pot of coffee and started to cook a meal of beans and ham. Slocum thought about demanding that they talk business before getting chummy, but the coffee and the food sure did smell good. He kept quiet.

And he did feel pretty safe. They had not lied about the layout. The view from the cabin was vast. He had been able to tell that, even in the moonlight. He would be able to see anyone coming long before he would arrive.

And no one else had been waiting at the cabin. At least it had not been that kind of trap.

"Coffee'll be ready in a minute," Jill said. "Oh. I wasn't thinking. Maybe you'd like something a little stronger."

She produced a bottle of brown whiskey from a cabinet on the wall and held it out for Slocum to see.

"That looks just fine," he said.

She brought it to him with a glass, and he poured himself a drink. The first swallow burned all the way down. It felt fine. He'd had two drinks by the time the food was on the table, and then the three of them sat down to eat. She could cook, too. Finished with the meal, Slocum poured himself another drink.

"Now," he said, "just what's this all about?"

"Our father is Brett Hooley," said Jill. "I guess his is the biggest ranch in these parts."

"It is the biggest," said Billy.

"I've heard of it," said Slocum, "even in the short time I've been here."

"We've been losing cattle lately," Jill continued. "Can't figure out who's getting them, or when, or where. And there's more. We've seen evidence of someone prowling around in the pass below here, down on the backside of this hill."

"Could be the rustlers," said Slocum.

"I don't think so," said Billy. "Someone was down there with a wagon a while back, and the cattle were all over on the other side of the ranch."

"Some pilgrim passing through," said Slocum.

"The tracks came in and went out the same way," said Jill. "No. There's something going on, and we think it's more than cattle rustling. For one thing, the rustling's not a big operation. It's more like whoever's doing it is just trying to annoy us."

"Say," said Slocum, "if Brett Hooley's your daddy, how do you come to be working in that joint in town?"

Jill blushed and ducked her head.

"That's got nothing to do with what we're talking about," she said. "It's personal between me and Papa."

Slocum took a sip of whiskey.

"Okay," he said. "So someone's making off with a few cows, and someone's been snooping around out here. What's that got to do with me and with the killing of Rolfe Wade?"

"Rolfe worked for us until about a week ago," said Billy. "He come riding hard into the bunkhouse late one evening and packed up his gear. Asked for his pay and said he quit."

"We thought it was pretty strange," said Jill. "We all got along real well with Rolfe, Papa included. Rolfe had been down in the pass that day. He wouldn't give us a reason for quitting, and he acted real nervous. Well, we kind of forgot about it in few days, and the talk around town was that he was getting ready to pull up stakes and head west. Then he got in that fight with you, and then someone killed him."

"You think maybe he saw something out here that day that got him killed?" Slocum asked.

"That's what we think," said Billy.

"And that's why we don't believe that you killed Rolfe," said Jill.

"Your problem and ours is tied together," Billy said.

"I see," said Slocum.

"Well?" said Jill. "Will you stay and help us?"

"I'll think it over for a day or two," said Slocum, "unless I see that posse headed my way."

7

Jill headed back toward Drownding Creek that same night, and Billy headed back for the ranch house. They didn't want anyone to suspect them of anything, and it seemed best that they each show up for work the next morning as if nothing was amiss in their lives. Slocum not only understood, he agreed.

Jill and Billy seemed to have a good reason for what they had done, and Slocum's mind was at ease as far as they were concerned. He no longer believed that it was possible that they had broken him out of jail to lead him into some kind of trap.

He believed their story. At least, he believed that they believed it. He wasn't at all sure that a few stolen cows and some wagon tracks meant that something sinister was going on. Any big rancher could expect to lose a few head now and then, and the wagon tracks could be explained any number of ways. Maybe someone had just lost his way.

Rolfe Wade's actions just a few days before his murder were curious, but they did not necessarily have anything to do with either the cows or the wagon tracks.

Even so, Slocum could well understand how the brother and sister had tied those things together in their minds, and therefore why they had busted him out of jail and were asking for his help.

He slept reasonably well that night with his mind at rest regarding the Hooleys. The bed was comfortable. The whiskey helped. Mostly it was because he was out of the jail cell and a safe distance away from Drownding Creek. At least it seemed so.

In the morning, he got up, dressed, and went outside to feed and water his horse. The air was nippy and invigorating. He looked out in all directions, and he was surprised to discover that he could actually see Drownding Creek.

He was not such a safe distance away, after all. Of course, the fact that he could see all that way made a difference. What the Hooleys had said was true. If a posse rode out of Drownding Creek in his direction, he could see them long before they would arrive, and he would have plenty of time to get away.

He realized, though, that any riders coming would see the smoke rising from the chimney of the line shack, and they might become suspicious and decide to investigate. He thought about putting the fire out, but he needed it to cook on, and the nights were starting to get cold. He decided to let it be and take his chances.

Looking out behind the cabin, there were rough hills, and that was the only direction in which he could not see almost forever. It was highly unlikely, though, that anyone would sneak up on him from there. The way would be up the hillside from the pass below, and the way into the pass from town was across the vast, open flatland. He felt secure enough to go back inside and cook himself a breakfast.

When he had finished eating, he went out again and saddled his horse. He wanted to ride down into the pass and take a look around. Slocum went down the front side of the hill, the way they had come, and then rode around to find the way into the pass. The wagon tracks were still there. He turned to look back, and it appeared that the wagon had come from Drownding Creek. He followed the tracks on into the pass.

Slocum estimated that he had ridden about half-way through the pass when he found the place were the wagon had turned around to go back out. The Hooleys were right. It was a puzzle. Why would anyone from Drownding Creek hitch up a wagon and drive out onto the Hooley ranch and into this pass, only to turn around and drive back again?

They might have been looking for something, but what? It must have been something that would require a wagon to take it back with them. Or they might have come to hide something. They might have used the wagon to bring something into the pass rather than take something out. Stolen money? A body? Then again, he thought, it might have been a pair of lovers looking for a good place to hide in order to keep their activities secret.

He decided that he wanted to talk to the Hooleys

a little more about this puzzle before snooping around for himself. He still felt a little like a fool for riding around in the open, not more than ten miles from Drownding Creek, having just broken out of its jail.

It was midmorning when Billy rode up to the cabin. Slocum had some coffee on, and Billy helped himself to a cup, then sat down at the table. Slocum sat across from him.

"I went into town with Papa this morning," Billy said. "He went to talk to the sheriff. He said too many strange things have been going on around here, and Bryce didn't seem to be doing anything about it. First, he said, there's the missing cattle.

"Bryce said that he'd been investigating, but these things take time. He said that in a case like this where just a few cows are stole every now and then, they might not ever catch up with the rustlers.

"Then there's that business about someone sneaking around on the ranch, Papa said. Driving a wagon out and snooping. Bryce said it might be the rustlers, and he was looking into it, but he's awful busy. He had a jail break to worry about just now, he said.

"He said two men had knocked Charlie on the head and broke a killer out of his jail last night."

"He's wrong on two counts there," said Slocum. "It wasn't the killer that got broke out, and it wasn't two men that broke him out. But that last part is good. It means they don't suspect you and Jill."

"Yeah," said Billy. "Anyhow, Papa said that there was the rest of it. He said something had scared Rolfe Wade into quitting him, and then a week later someone had murdered Rolfe. They put the killer in jail—that's what Papa said—and then someone breaks him out again."

"It sounds like your papa figures all these events are tied together," said Slocum.

"He does, but he can't convince Bryce. But Papa's got it figured wrong, Slocum. He said that you was likely the rustler, and that Wade had probably seen you out here in the pass. That's why you had that fight, and that's why you killed Wade. That's what Papa said.

"Course, old Bryce, he asked Papa when he first missed any cattle, and when Papa told him, Bryce said that you hadn't been around these parts that long. He said you couldn't be the rustler."

"Be damned," said Slocum. "I figured that Bryce would hang anything he could on me."

"Well, he still thinks you killed Wade, and Papa still thinks the other way. He told Bryce that maybe you had come in later and then joined up with the others. He said we know that there's more than one because two of them came around to break him out of jail. Course we know better than that, but I couldn't very well tell Papa or Bryce."

"No. You couldn't," said Slocum. "Did Bryce say anything about tracking me with a posse?"

"He followed the tracks out of town this morning for a ways and then lost them," said Billy. "He rode a couple of circles around town trying to pick them up, but he didn't have no luck. He said he was going to search the town—every damn house and every damn business—and if he didn't find you that way, he was going to send out some men to scour the whole countryside."

"That ain't good," said Slocum. "They'll surely

come up this way. It's the best place to hide for miles around here."

"Maybe not. Last night when me and Jill rode out of here, we made tracks around the hills, like we had headed off toward the border. Besides, Bryce seen the smoke from the cabin here, and he asked if we was using this old place. I told him that I was using it. I was afraid Papa would say something, but he never."

Slocum got up and poured himself a cup of coffee, then went back to the table.

"Billy," he said, "have there been any other killings around here lately?"

"No. Not since Joe Biggers shot Tom Conley out in the middle of the street in front of God and everybody. They stretched Joe's neck for it, too."

"When was that?"

"Must have been six months ago."

"Any robberies?"

"You mean besides our cattle?"

"Yeah."

"Nothing I heard about. How come?"

"Oh, probably nothing," said Slocum. I'm just thinking about that wagon. Seems to me it either came into the pass to haul something out or to bring something in and hide it."

"Oh," said Billy. "Well, I can't think of nothing anyone'd be hiding."

"Yeah," said Slocum. He bit his lip and mused for a moment. "Billy," he said, "you think you could find an excuse for spending the day over here tomorrow?"

"Sure," said Billy. "How come?"

"If I ain't up here on top," said Slocum, "where I

can see, I'm nervous about that posse. I'd like for you to be here to keep watch while I roam around down there in the pass awhile. See what I can see."

"I'll be here," said Billy. "You'll have all the time you want."

Billy rode on out shortly after that, and Slocum spent the rest of the morning and afternoon thinking and figuring. He didn't come up with anything.

The sun was almost down when Slocum heard the sound of an approaching horse. He grabbed his Winchester and pressed himself against the wall beside a window. Then he saw Jill riding up. He leaned the rifle against the wall and opened the door. Jill dismounted and hurried into the cabin.

"You're still here," she said.

"Told you I would be," said Slocum, "lessen I seen that posse coming. I ain't seen it yet."

"Me and Billy tried to throw them off with our tracks last night," she said.

"I know," he said. "Billy told me."

"You seen Billy today?"

"He came by for a spell," said Slocum, "but what are you doing out here? You ought to stay clear of me. So far, no one suspects you of being involved in that breakout."

"I know," she said. "Charlie said two men slipped up on him, and he couldn't identify either one of them. Don't worry. No one's going to come searching out here this late in the day. I just thought you might like someone's cooking for supper other than your own."

"I can't turn that down," said Slocum. He lit a cigar and poured himself a whiskey, as Jill went to the stove to get the meal started. Slocum sat down at the table. He was mostly looking at her back, and she was wearing jeans and a man's shirt. He thought that her ass sure did fill the backside of those jeans nicely.

"What'd you find to do around here all day?" she asked over her shoulder.

"Not much," said Slocum. "I rode down into the pass this morning for a quick look. That's about it."

"So what did you find down there?"

"Nothing much. No more than what you had already told me, but I mean to go back and spend some real time at it. Your brother said he'd come and stand watch for me tomorrow while I'm down there."

"That's a good idea," she said, and she dropped something into a hot skillet that sizzled loudly. "You have any idea what you'll be looking for?"

"Other than a reason for someone to drive a wagon in there," said Slocum, "no. How about you?"

"I've tried and tried to think of something," she said. "Me and Billy together. We ain't come up with a thing."

Slocum watched her move, and he liked what he saw. Whenever she took a step in any direction, her hips swayed seductively. He told himself that she wasn't doing that on purpose. It was just the way a woman moved. And her visit to the cabin and cooking this meal was nothing more than business. She wanted to make sure that he was staying around to help them crack this puzzle. That was all, and he had no intention of making a fool out of himself by making a pass at her.

She turned and slid a plate across the table in front of him. It was covered with brown beans, fried potatoes, and fried thick slabs of bacon.

"I'll try to bring you some fresh steak tomorrow," she said.

"Thanks," he said. "This looks fine."

"You want some coffee?"

He held up his whiskey glass.

"This is all I need," he said. "Listen. I appreciate this, but you're going to wear yourself out. You couldn't have got much sleep last night, and here you are out here again. You've got a long ride back to town, and you have to be up early for work. I like your company, but don't you think you'd ought to head on back?"

She sat down across the table from him and looked him in the eyes.

"I think I ought to head on back," she said, "or else plan to stay the night and get an early start in the morning. What do you think?"

8

Slocum stopped eating. He looked straight at Jill, sitting there across the table from him, her big, brown eyes staring at him seductively. He had just gotten one hell of an invitation, and he could hardly believe his luck. She was young, and she was gorgeous. He hadn't even made a move on her, and here she had actually offered herself to him. And he had already been fantasizing about her in both his night and day dreams. Now here she was, offering to make those dreams come true. But something about it did not feel right to Slocum.

"Jill," he said, and he could scarcely believe himself as he said it. "Go on back to town. Tonight."

He read the look of disbelief on her face, and

he could see that it was about to turn to indignation and maybe even wrath. He could imagine what she was thinking, for she had just made him a most generous offer, and he was refusing her. And a refusal of that kind was more than most women could take. He had to give her some sort of an explanation to convince her that his response was not an insult, and that her offer was really appreciated, in spite of his response.

"I'll kick myself all night long for what I'm saying to you," he continued, "and if you ever make the same offer again, believe me, I won't turn you down. But for right now I want you to get a few things clear in your mind and then have a little time to think it all over.

"First off, I ain't likely to be staying around these parts. I ain't even made up my mind about staying long enough to straighten this mess out, like you want me to do. Hell. First time I see a posse headed this direction, I might just hightail it out of here.

"Remember now, I ain't made you no promises. And I wouldn't want to think you was doing—what you'd be doing—just to convince me to hang around. On the other hand, I wouldn't want you to get no wrong ideas about my intentions, either."

Jill stood up almost immediately, and left in a huff without saying another word, and Slocum thought that she might come back the next time slinging lead at him. He thought again that maybe he ought to just get the hell out of there and ride as far away from Drownding Creek and the Hooley Ranch as his Appaloosa would carry him.

Instead, he poured himself a glass of whiskey and

sat down again, musing on the marvelous pleasures he had just denied himself and calling himself ten times a God damned do-gooder fool.

"You've done taken up store keeping," he said out loud. "What's next? Sunday school teaching?"

Slocum slept well that night, once he got to sleep, and as usual, he was awake early the next morning. He rolled over in bed and noticed through the window on the wall across the room a reddish glow low in the sky. For a moment, his senses still dull from sleep, he thought it was the sunrise. Then he remembered that the cabin did not face east, and the window was in the front wall. He came awake at once and sprang out of bed, rushing across the room to take a look.

It was a few miles away, but he knew what it was. He didn't know exactly which building, but something was burning at the Hooley Ranch headquarters. He thought briefly about rushing over there to help, but he quickly rejected that idea. He would be seen, and the chances that word would get back to the sheriff in Drownding Creek were pretty damn good.

Besides, he told himself, he really wasn't needed over there. The biggest ranch in these parts surely had a big crew. One more really wouldn't make all that much difference. And the flames were high. Whatever was burning was already a loss, anyhow. The firefighters would be mostly trying to keep the flames from spreading to other structures.

He got dressed and spent most of the morning watching the fire. His plan to go down in the pass was shot, because it depended on the presence of

Billy up on the hill, and Billy was surely busy with the fire.

Slocum estimated that it was close to two o'clock in the afternoon when Billy finally came riding up to the cabin. He stepped outside to meet the young man.

"Howdy," he said. "Looked like you had some trouble this morning."

"Yeah," said Billy, dismounting. "You seen it from here?"

"Couldn't miss it."

"Well, that's why I didn't show like I said I would."

"When I saw them flames," said Slocum, "I knew I wouldn't be seeing you for awhile. Want to come on inside?"

"Yeah."

They went in, and Billy sat down at the table.

"You want some coffee?" Slocum asked. "A drink or anything?"

"No," said Billy. "Thanks."

"What burned?"

"The barn," said Billy. "It started sometime before daylight. By the time anyone knew about it, it was too late to save it."

"How did it start?" Slocum asked. "Could you tell?"

"Not really," said young Hooley, "but Papa says he's sure that someone started it on purpose."

"That makes sense," said Slocum.

"How do you mean?"

"Well, we figured that someone was rustling your cows mainly as an annoyance, didn't we?"

"Yeah."

"Whoever it is just decided to annoy you a little harder."

"Damn," said Billy. He stood up and paced across the room to the window and stood there for a moment with his back to Slocum. Then he turned to face him again. "But why?"

"I reckon the answer might be down there in that pass," said Slocum. "Someone's been down there with a wagon, and no one can figure why. Wade was out this way the day he rode back in all nervous and up and quit your outfit. Then just about a week later, someone killed him. I'm mighty curious about that pass."

"Yeah," said Billy. "Me, too. Try again tomorrow morning?"

"I'd say so."

Billy headed for the door.

"I'll see you then," he said, "unless we wake up with another big surprise."

Slocum spent the rest of that day feeding himself and his horse and pacing around the cabin. He was beginning to feel caged up again. True, the cage was more pleasant than the last one, and the company, when he had company, was a whole lot more sociable, but still he wasn't really free. He was hiding out, skulking, and he didn't like it a bit.

He fought off a powerful urge to saddle the Appaloosa, steal a few supplies for the trail, including what was left of the whiskey, and start riding west. He told himself that the Hooleys' problems were none of his concern, that he was a fool for hanging around the ranch so close to Drownding Creek. The longer he stayed around, the higher the chances of

Bryce finding out where he was hiding and picking him up again.

Hell, he hadn't known these people but a few days, and here he was risking his neck for them like a damn fool. But then it came to him that they were, after all, pretty nice folks, and he also admitted to himself that without them, he would still be sitting in that damned jail cell down in Drownding Creek with a hell of a good chance of being tried for murder and found guilty and maybe even hanged. He guessed that he owed them something.

If he could actually help them solve the mystery of their problems on the ranch, he couldn't be sure, but he had a powerful feeling that along the way he would also prove that someone else had killed old Wade. Something told him that all these events were related. So if he was right about that, solving their problem would also solve his. He'd still ride away from this damned country, but he wouldn't have to run away.

And then there was Jill. After what he had said to her the night before, he could not deny that he was real curious whether or not she would make her offer again. He was even hoping that she would. He had told her that he would not turn her down twice, and by God, he had meant it. He wondered if she would come back that evening to fix him another supper. By sundown, he realized that she would not.

When Billy Hooley showed up the next morning, Slocum was more than ready to go. He had been cooped up about as long as he could stand it, so he just told Billy to keep a sharp eye and come riding down into the pass to warn him if he saw anyone headed their way, especially anyone from Drownding Creek.

The Appaloosa was already saddled up, so Slocum climbed onto his back and headed down the hill. He rode around to the entrance to the pass the same way he had before, and, as before, he followed the wagon tracks until they turned to go back out the way they had come in. It was as big a puzzle as ever.

Slocum dismounted and walked over to the base of the wall of the pass. It was not a cliff wall. It was a steep hillside, and it was covered with thick brush and scrawny trees. In between the trees and behind and under the brush were some big boulders. It was rough ground.

Slocum poked around for awhile, trying to find some indication of where someone might have gone into the brush, but he found nothing. *Well,* he thought, *they wouldn't have got out of the wagon and walked any farther into the pass to do whatever it was they was doing, but they might have done something along the way, before they drove on up here and turned around.*

He climbed back into the saddle and rode slowly back the way he had come in, staying close to the edge and watching carefully as he rode. He had gone maybe a hundred yards when he noticed something almost imperceptible. He very nearly rode past it. He wasn't even sure that it was anything, but it called for a closer look.

He dismounted and squatted there at the edge of the brushy rise. Someone had gone through there. He was sure. It had not been too recently, but whenever it had happened, it had been more than once. The brambles there were mashed back in an unnatural way, and the wall there was much too steep for cattle to have caused the disturbance.

He fought his way through the thick, matted tangle and climbed the steep hillside for a way, and then all of a sudden he found himself on a relatively clear path. At this point, the brush had been hacked away to make a trail. It was still steep, and the climb was not an easy one, but at least there was nothing to get tangled up in along the way. He kept going.

About a quarter of the way up, he came to a narrow ledge, and he sat down to take a breather. He noticed that the trail did not turn to follow the ledge but continued straight up. He decided that he'd rested up enough, and was about the get to his feet to resume the climb, when he saw the butt of a tailor-made cigarette lying there on the ledge.

"Well, I'll be damned," he said. He picked the butt up and studied it for a moment, then dropped it into his shirt pocket. Someone else had stopped on the ledge to take a break. He looked around some more but saw nothing else of interest. He started to climb again.

He had gone about as far again and estimated himself to be about halfway up the hill when he came to another ledge, and here there was yet another surprise. The ledge was wider than the one below, and it showed evidence of having been widened by the actions of man. He also found two more cigarette butts on the ledge, but even that was not the big surprise.

Standing up on the ledge and facing the hillside, Slocum was looking into the mouth of a dark cave or tunnel.

9

Billy Hooley was practically hopping up and down with anticipation when he saw Slocum come riding back up toward the cabin. Of course, he didn't know whether Slocum had actually found anything or not, but he had high hopes, and besides, he was bored with waiting and watching alone. It was already the middle of the afternoon, and it had been a long and slow day for young Billy.

"What did you find?" he yelled.

Slocum rode slowly on up to the cabin and pulled the big, spotted horse to a halt.

"Howdy yourself," he said, as he swung down out of the saddle.

"Howdy," said Billy. "What did you find down there? Anything? You were sure gone a long time."

"Yeah," said Slocum, "it's been a long damn day, and I'm hungry. Let me at least take care of my horse and then get myself something to eat. Then we'll talk."

"Well, all right," said Billy. "I'll rustle you up some grub."

Slocum wiped his plate almost clean with what was left of a cold biscuit, stuffed the soppy bread into his mouth, and swallowed it down. Then he finished off the coffee in his cup, pushed himself back away from the table, and went over to the cabinet for the whiskey bottle. He poured himself a drink, carried it back to the table, and sat down again.

"Well, I think I know what it is that's been going on around here, Billy," he said.

"What?" said Billy. "What is it? What did you find out?"

Slocum took a casual sip of his whiskey.

"Has anyone offered to buy the ranch lately?" he asked.

Billy looked thoughtful for a moment and scratched his head.

"Well," he said, "not for a couple of months, and then it wasn't no serious offer."

"Tell me about it," said Slocum.

"Old Basil Reid came up to the house one day, like I said, a couple of months ago, and he asked Papa to name a price. Papa said the place ain't for sale. Basil argued with him a little, said anything's got a price tag on it, but Papa wouldn't budge. Pretty soon Basil rode on out again. That's all. Funny thing is, Basil ain't got no money. Not that kind of money, anyhow."

"Who is this Basil Reid?" Slocum asked.

Billy shrugged.

"He has the look of a cowboy," he said, "but he ain't rode for no ranch in these parts. Not that I know of. He just kind of hangs around. Got friendly with Rolfe Wade about the time Rolfe quit us."

"That's interesting," said Slocum. "Do you know if this Reid fellow smokes tailor-mades?"

"I never noticed. I don't know. Why?"

"What about Wade?"

"No," said Billy. "I never seen Wade smoke at all. He chewed."

Slocum pulled the butts of the tailor-mades out of his shirt pocket and dropped them on the tabletop in front of Billy.

"I found these over there," he said, "where all the snooping's been going on. I found something else, too. You say you got no idea why anyone might be interested in that pass?"

"No," said Billy. "I sure can't figure it. Just what the hell did you find out there, anyway? You're making me crazy."

Slocum paused and sipped some more whiskey. He held the glass up to the light and studied the brown liquid for a brief moment.

"You can't see it unless you climb up to it," said Slocum, "but there's an old mine tunnel over there, dug straight into the hillside about halfway up. It looks to me like it ain't been worked in a long time, but someone's been snooping in there recent, and whoever it was dug out some pretty good chunks for samples. I figure that's what the wagon was for. To carry out the samples they stole."

"What kind of samples?" Billy asked.

"Gold, Billy boy," said Slocum. "Gold."

"Gold?" Billy repeated, incredulous. "You mean—"

"I mean you've got a rich gold mine just on the other side of this hill. Hell, we might be sitting on a whole mountain of gold."

Billy's eyes were wide. He stood up and paced across the floor.

"Well, I'll be God damned," he said. "I'll be kiss my ass. A mountain of gold."

"It all comes clear, Billy," said Slocum. "All except who's to blame. But I'd bet my horse that Reid is in on it, and Wade was, too. Only there's got to be someone else, someone with money."

"What do you mean?" said Billy, moving back to the table to sit.

"Well," said Slocum. "Here's how I've got it figured. Someone around here found out about that old mine, and whoever that person is wants to get this ranch away from your daddy. You said that Reid ain't got the money, yet he asked for a price. So that means he's likely fronting for the man with the money. And since your daddy is firm about not wanting to sell, the rustling and the fire are all intended to soften him up. Give him enough trouble, and maybe he'll sell. Get it?"

"Yeah," said Billy. "I see. Damn. A gold mine. Well, what do we do now? Go after Reid?"

"I don't know," said Slocum. "I ain't sure, but I don't think so. Not just yet. Hell, we can't prove nothing on him except that he asked your old man for a price on the ranch. There's no crime in that. No, I think we need to just find a way of watching this Reid for awhile. See if we can find out who he might be chummy with who's got the kind of money it would take to buy this place if it was for sale."

"Jill can do that," said Billy. "She's in town all the time anyway, and she sees a lot of folks there in Rosie's every day."

"Can you ride in and see her today?" Slocum asked.

"Sure."

"Good. Tell her to watch Reid, and tell her to look out for anyone who smokes those damn sissified factory-made cigarettes. There can't be very many of them around. Hell, old Crocker don't even stock them in his store."

"Okay," said Billy. "I'll go in right now."

"Billy," said Slocum. "Be careful. Don't let anyone hear you talking to Jill about this, and tell Jill to be careful, too. Tell her not to do anything, but only keep her eyes open. That's all. If she learns anything, tell her to get out here or over to the ranch house and tell either you or me about it. Men will kill over gold. These, whoever they are, have done killed Wade."

"You think that's why Wade was killed?"

"I think Wade knew about the gold," Slocum said. "He might even be the one who found it. He worked out here. Maybe he found that old tunnel somehow, and he didn't want to tell your daddy about it. After all, it wouldn't have done him no good.

"So instead, he went to someone else, someone with money, and told him. He probably offered to show this money man the tunnel, or some samples from it to prove that it existed, and then made some kind of deal with him. If they could get the ranch, then Wade would get a share in the mine, even though he didn't have any cash to put in on the deal.

Then they had some kind of falling out. Maybe old Wade got greedy and threatened to tell your old man if he didn't get a better deal or something. Tell Jill to be careful."

"I will," said Billy.

"And Billy."

"Yeah?"

"I don't know your old man. Do you think we ought to let him in on this? Tell him what all we know?"

"I don't know, Slocum," said Billy. "He was convinced that you was in on the rustling. I'll ask Jill before I say anything to Papa. See what she thinks about it."

As Billy rode down the hill, Slocum pondered the situation he was in. He had the law after him on the one side, and on the other he was setting himself up against at least two men, maybe more, and they were almost for certain killers. And for allies, he had only Billy and Jill Hooley on his side. It didn't look good.

Billy was only about halfway down the hill when he turned around and hurried back to the cabin. Slocum heard him coming and stepped outside. As soon as he did, he saw why Billy had returned so quickly.

"Sheriff's coming," said Billy.

"I see him," said Slocum. "Just one man with him."

"It's Charlie," said Billy. "What're we going to do?"

"I'll take your horse around to the corral," said Slocum. "You go inside and act like everything's normal. Try to keep them away from the corral. If they come out there and find me, I'll have to shoot."

Slocum took Billy's horse and disappeared around

the cabin, and Billy hurried inside. He looked around quickly to see if there was anything of Slocum's out in sight. There were saddlebags, a blanket, an extra shirt, and the Winchester.

He grabbed them all up and stuffed them under the bed. Then he stacked the dirty dishes and cups in the dish pan. At the last minute, as he heard the horses approaching just outside, he noticed the cigarette butts lying there on the table where Slocum had tossed them, and he scooped them up and dropped them into his shirt pocket. Then he went to the door and opened it. Bryce and Charlie had just stopped their horses.

"Hello, sheriff," Billy said. "Charlie. Come on in. I've got some coffee on. It ain't too fresh, but it's strong."

"Don't mind if I do," said Bryce. "Come on, Charlie."

The two lawmen dismounted and followed Billy inside. They sat at the table as Billy poured them each a cup of coffee and brought the cups to them at the table.

"What brings you up this way?" he asked.

"We're out looking around for that Slocum," said Bryce. "You told me you was staying up here. I just thought I'd drop in and ask had you seen anything. You've got a hell of a view from up here."

"Well, I ain't seen nothing of Slocum," said Billy. "Ain't seen much of anything. Been watching for some sign of them rustlers, you know. No luck so far."

"I'd sure like to get my hands on that son of a bitch," said Charlie. "I've still got a scabby lump on my head where his buddy busted my skull."

He reached into his shirt pocket and pulled out a box from which he removed a tailor-made cigarette. He put the cigarette between his lips and returned the box to his pocket.

"You got a match?" he asked.

Billy tore his eyes away from the telltale smoke and got up from the table.

"Sure," he said.

He brought a tin of matches back and tossed them on the table in front of Charlie. Charlie lit his cigarette.

"Say," said Billy. "I never seen any of them kind of smokes before. They any good?"

Charlie pulled the box out of his pocket again and tossed it at Billy.

"Try one," he said.

"Thanks."

Billy lit a cigarette, drew deeply on it, and let out a cloud of smoke.

"Not bad," he said. "Where do you get these things?"

"Emporium in town," said Charlie. "If you start buying them though, you tell Marvin to order some extra ones. He only gets them in for me. They ain't too popular, you know."

"Oh. Sure. I'll tell him," said Billy. "Have you been down to the ranch house today?"

"Yeah," said Bryce. "We stopped in to see your pa. He didn't have anything new for us, and we didn't have anything for him. Too bad about the barn."

"Someone set that fire," said Billy.

"Maybe," said Bryce. "We got no proof."

"No other way it could have started."

"We still got no proof."

Bryce drained his cup and stood up.

"We better move on," he said. "We still got a lot of ground to cover. I can't figure out how that damn Slocum could have disappeared the way he did."

"We'll find the bastard," said Charlie, "and his buddies."

"Yeah," said Billy. "Well, I'll keep my eyes open. Good luck."

He followed them outside and watched as they rode down the hill. When they had disappeared, he heard Slocum step up behind him.

"They suspect anything?" Slocum asked.

"They didn't seem to," said Billy, "but looky here."

He turned and held the still-burning, tailor-made cigarette out toward Slocum. Slocum took it and looked at it more closely. Then he looked at Billy, questioning.

"Charlie," said Billy. "The Emporium orders them just for him."

10

It was almost dark when Jill rode up to the cabin. Slocum had heard the horse and was waiting at the doorway with his Winchester ready. When he saw her, he leaned the rifle against the wall, opened the door, and stepped back out of the way.

"I wasn't looking for you," he said.

"You ain't glad to see me?"

"Sure I am."

"It's too late for me to ride back to town tonight," she said.

"I'll take care of your horse," he said.

Back inside, sitting across the table from her, Slocum tried to figure this young woman out. Her arrival at the cabin at that late hour and her own comment about it made it clear that she had come to spend the night with him. Did she indeed find him attractive, in spite of the difference in their ages? Or was there some other explanation for her behavior?

"Did Billy go into town to see you?" he asked.

"Yeah," she said. "He told me what you found, and he said that you've got it all figured out except for who's behind it."

"Well, I think so," he said. "I know what it looks like, but we can't prove much of anything."

"Except that Charlie's been snooping around on our property," she said.

"I ain't even sure that we got absolute proof there," said Slocum. "A slick lawyer would say that someone else could have smoked them cigarettes."

"So where do we go from here?"

"I think we need a list of everyone in town, or anywhere close around, who has the kind of money it would take to buy a spread like this," said Slocum. "That would at least give us something to start with. Then we watch real close to see who Charlie and that other fellow—what was his name?"

"Basil Reid?"

"Yeah. The fellow who tried to buy the ranch. We get this list of folks with money and then we watch to see who on that list Reid or Charlie spend any time with."

"That could take a lot of time," said Jill. She stood up and walked over to the cabinets in the area of the cabin that served as a kitchen. "You had your supper?" she asked.

"No. I ain't."

"Me, neither. I'll fix us some."

"Thanks," said Slocum. "You know, I'm pretty

strapped up here. It seems to me that it would help us a whole bunch if your daddy knew what we're up to and was working with us."

"Billy said something about that," said Jill.

"What do you think?"

"I'll go talk to him first thing in the morning," she said.

"What about your job?"

"I quit just before I rode out this way," she said.

"Oh."

While Jill finished preparing the meal, Slocum smoked a cigar. He tried to think out what their strategy should be if old man Hooley was working with them. There was, of course, a danger to Slocum in letting the old man in on their activities. In spite of the assurances of his children, he could still believe that Slocum was a part of the mysterious opposition and turn him in to the sheriff.

But if that happened, Slocum told himself, he would still be able to see a posse coming from town and have time to get away. Then he realized that if the old man were to rat on Slocum, he would also have to turn his own kids in for breaking Slocum out of jail. He wouldn't want to do that. Slocum decided that it was probably safe for them to tell the old man.

Jill put the meal on the table, and they ate. Then they each had a glass of whiskey. Slocum noticed that Jill sipped hers and took it pretty well, but it raised a blush on her cheeks. For the first time in days, Slocum did not want to get the hell out of the cabin.

"I'm sorry I huffed out of here the other night," she said. "It was really good of you to say what you did. I realized that, after I thought about it awhile."

"You don't need to apologize," he said. "Hell, some women would have taken a shot at me."

"I thought about it," she said, and they both laughed. Slocum downed the rest of the whiskey in his glass and reached for the bottle. He held it up toward Jill, as if to ask if she wanted a refill.

"No thanks," she said. "I don't need no more."

She stood up and started walking around the table toward Slocum. His eyes on her all the way, he put the bottle back down on the table, not bothering to refill his own glass. Something even better than whiskey was on the way.

She stopped close by his chair and, looking down at him, began slowly to unfasten the buttons of her shirt front. Slocum watched for a moment before he reached up and took her by the wrists, stopping her.

"This ain't out of gratitude or anything like that, is it?" he asked her.

"Do we have to go through that again?" she said.

"No," he said. He stood up and put his arms around her, pulling her close and holding her tight for a long, quiet moment. With his right hand, he stroked her back, then rubbed her neck and finally tangled his fingers in her hair. When he at last relaxed his grip, she moved back just enough to lift her face toward his, and he kissed her on the lips, gently, tenderly at first, then harder and more passionately.

Then she pulled herself away from him and, taking his hand, led him to the bed. They undressed slowly, standing there facing one another, each one watching the other drop one item of clothing after another onto the floor, each one watching the other's body revealed just that much more with each discarded item. At last they stood naked, face to face.

Jill's eyes moved down to see the swollen cock, already risen and ready for action, and she could not take her eyes away. Slocum reached forward to take a lovely breast in each hand, and his thumbs flicked back and forth across the nipples, causing them to harden and swell. He could hear her breathing quicken.

His hands slid around to her smooth back and pulled her close, and she could feel the throbbing rod against her belly. She moaned as she pressed herself against him, and his hands slid down to grip the round cheeks of her tight ass.

They kissed again, this time dueling with their tongues and pressing their mouths hard against one another. He guided her, their tongues still lapping greedily at the inside of each other's mouths, to a sitting position on the edge of the bed, and then he laid her back.

She spread her legs wide as he moved between them, still up on his knees, and she reached down with both her hands to grip his cock and balls. The cock throbbed and bucked in her hand, like a thing alive with its own mind, trying to escape. She held it hard.

Slocum put a hand on the hairy mound of her crotch and pressed it, feeling its warmth, and one finger found the slit and moved between the luscious lips into the wetness there. He drove the finger in as deeply as he could, and she humped against it, moaning. Their lips had not yet parted. Their tongues still lapped at one another almost viciously.

She started to pull his cock, guiding it toward her anxious cunt, drawing him down toward her with it, using it as a handle to put him where she wanted him. He moved his hand away from her crotch and allowed himself to be pulled downward, and she found the channel and rubbed the cock head up and down a few times in almost desperate movements before she put it there in just the right place, thrusting upward with her hips. Slocum pressed downward at the same time, driving his full length deep into her.

"Oh," she cried out loud, but she continued pressing up against him, holding the cock in deep, feeling it jump and throb inside her. She dug her nails into the cheeks of his ass, and then she squeezed him with the walls of her cunt. She relaxed a little, and Slocum pulled back, withdrawing, almost slipping out before he drove it deep again. Then they began moving together, beautifully, as if they had both been made for just this act.

Slocum pulled his mouth away from hers at last and dropped his head beside hers and breathed heavily, panted, into her ear, as down below they both continued driving and humping their bodies together to the sounds of squishing and slapping below and panting and moaning above.

Harder and faster they pounded away, both bodies now drenched with sweat, and then she came. Her motion stopped with an upward thrust. Her back was arched as if she were trying to lift him up off the bed, and she gripped him hard again by the cheeks of his ass and pulled him against her with all her strength.

Her moan turned almost to a pitiful cry, and she held him hard and whimpered for a long moment, before she finally, slowly, relaxed her grip on him and allowed her own body to sink back down into the bed.

Slocum drew his knees up under him, at the same time spreading them and lifting her legs. He wound up sitting on his knees, her ass nestled between his thighs, her legs sticking straight up in front of him, his cock still deep inside her. He rubbed her legs and kissed her calves, and then he started driving in and out again. She rolled her head to one side and smiled, enjoying the sensation.

She bent her knees and pressed the soles of her feet against his chest, as he drove harder and faster, and he watched her breasts bounce each time he slammed against her. He could feel the welling up and the pressure building deep inside him. He forced himself to slow his strokes. He wasn't ready for this to end.

Pushing gently on her legs, he laid her over on her side, at the same time lying down just behind her, his chest against her back, her ass pressing into his belly, his arm around her, squeezing one ripe breast, his cock still deep inside her soppy cunt. He kissed her on the neck. She moaned and rocked her rump back into him. He pressed against her for a moment, enjoying the feeling of this new position, savoring each delicate curve of her body, and then he started to hump again, and she moved with him.

He felt the pressure building up again, and so again he slowed his strokes. He stopped, and he raised himself to his knees, pulling her along with him, until she was on her hands and knees and he was kneeling behind her. He gripped her by the hips and started pounding into her hard and fast.

"Ah. Ah. Ah."

With each thrust she moaned, and she lowered her head and shoulder down onto the bed, thus thrusting her ass higher and freeing her hands at the same time. She reached back under her, between her legs, between his legs, and found his balls and gripped them with both hands, and Slocum almost shouted out.

A stream burst forth and flooded her insides. He pulled back a little and thrust again, sending another gush into her. He kept pumping, but slower, and with each new thrust, he shot a little less. At last he was done. He held his position, still holding onto her hips, allowing his cock to soften inside her warm, wet cunt. When at last it slipped free, limp, spent, useless but smug and satisfied, Slocum turned and fell onto his back beside Jill with a long groan of pleasure.

Still on her knees, she looked at him and smiled.

"I can't believe I turned that down the other night," he said.

She snaked a hand over to fondle his soft but still swollen cock and balls.

"Ooh," she said. "You're all wet and sticky. You need a cleaning."

She left him in the bed only to return a moment later with a dampened towel, and she crawled in from the foot of the bed, moving up between his legs. He felt a new sensation as she washed him there with the wet towel, and he was completely relaxed. He felt a deep sleep coming on.

Jill finished with the towel and dropped it to the floor. Then she curled herself into a ball, snuggling down between his wide-spread legs. She lay her head on his thigh so that her cheek was against his cock. There in the dim light, she looked at the thing that had just given her such intense pleasure. It looked completely helpless now.

She took hold of it and lifted it. Then she raised her head and kissed it with her lips. She rolled over on her belly there between his legs, holding the cock now in both her hands, and she put out her tongue and licked the head to taste it, and she felt it throb again. And Slocum was awake.

11

As much as Slocum was suffering from cabin fever and wanted to get the hell off the hilltop, he declined the offer of riding down to the ranch house with Jill the next morning as too risky. Even if old Hooley turned out to be agreeable, some of his ranch hands might spot Slocum and not feel the same way. He decided to tough it out and wait to see how Jill and Billy fared with their father.

Jill had fixed them a breakfast before she left, and Slocum had nothing more to do but smoke cigars, drink coffee, try to think things through, and wait. He thought that it was a hell of a situation to be in. Of course, he could just sit back and enjoy recalling the events of the past night. As it turned out, the morning was long for Slocum, and he did all of those things.

It was around noon, and Slocum was outside the cabin, staring off toward the ranch house, when he saw three riders coming toward the hill. When they came closer, he recognized Jill and Billy, and he relaxed a bit. The other rider, he guessed, was old man Hooley. He stood there and waited for them to arrive.

When they at last rode up in front of the cabin, the older man riding between the two youngsters stared hard at Slocum without saying a word. Billy dismounted and stepped toward Slocum.

"Slocum," he said, "this is our father, Brett Hooley. Papa, this here is John Slocum."

Jill jumped down out of the saddle.

"Let's go inside," she said.

"I'll take care of the horses," said Billy. Brett Hooley climbed down from his horse's back. Jill led the way into the cabin, followed by Slocum and Hooley. The man sat down in one of the chairs at the table.

"I've got coffee," said Slocum.

"I'll pour it," said Jill.

Slocum sat across from Hooley. The old man still looked hard and tough. He was medium height, but solid and stocky underneath his white hair.

"Slocum," he said, "I've got two hardheaded kids."

"I've noticed that," said Slocum.

"If I'd known what they were up to from the beginning on this deal, you'd still be sitting in that jail down there."

"I figured that, too."

"But I'm slowly learning not to interfere," the old man went on. "They're grown. Mostly. And they've got their own minds, and sometimes they're right in what they're thinking."

Jill put coffee cups all around the table, and just then Billy came in the door. He laid some saddlebags against the wall just inside the door. Then he took a chair at the table, and so did Jill.

"First off," Hooley said, "I guess you were arrested on a pretty flimsy excuse. Under normal circumstances, that's not a reason to bust a man out of jail. It's an argument to take to court. But the circumstances here are not normal. Not anywhere near it. Now, I've heard from these two, but I want to hear it from you. What have you found, and what do you make of it all?"

"Well," said Slocum, "it all started for me with the fight I had with Rolfe Wade. Wasn't much to it. I didn't even know the man. It started the way most fights start, I guess, over not much of anything, and I whipped him. Then I offered to buy him a drink, and he accepted.

"I was all ready to leave town the next morning, because I figured that Mr. Crocker was going to fire me anyhow for fighting with a customer, and besides, I ain't no storekeeper, and I had already had about all of it I could take, so I had packed my roll and moved out of his room at the back of the store.

"Anyhow, we went on over to the saloon and had a few drinks. Then I went—"

Slocum shot a glance at Jill, and Jill was looking down at the table. He continued.

"Well, I went on my way and left Wade there at the bar."

"Yes," said Hooley. "I know where you went. Never mind that part. Go on."

"That's the last I ever seen of Rolfe Wade," said Slocum. "The next morning, while I was having my breakfast in Rosie's and thinking to hit the road as soon as I'd looked up Crocker, Bryce and his two deputies walked up behind me and put the strong-arm to me. They locked me up and charged me with the murder of Wade. That was the first I knew that he'd been killed.

"Bryce said I'd fought with him, which was true, and that I couldn't prove where I was when he was killed. Well, I reckon that was true, too. He also said that my fixing to leave town made it look bad for me.

"I told him that I don't even own a shotgun, and he said that I could have easily used one out of the store. The next morning, Jill came around and told me to be ready. She said that she and her brother was fixing to bust me out of there. I didn't hardly know her, either, and I'd never heard of old Billy here, so that was a real puzzle to me.

"When they did get me out, they told me about all your troubles out here: losing cows, someone snooping around, and Wade quitting the way he done. They figured there was some connection between Wade's quitting, the troubles on the ranch, and his getting killed, and since I'd been accused of the killing, they thought that maybe I'd help them out some way. Maybe solve all of our problems at once, I guess."

"We didn't even know if he'd really stick around to help us," said Billy. "We just decided to go ahead and take a chance on him."

"You keep your mouth shut," said Hooley. "I've heard your story. I'm getting this now from Slocum. Go on, Slocum."

"Well, I checked out the wagon tracks, and I found

out why the snooping. There's an old shaft in the side of the hill over there. A gold mine. Someone's been in there recently and took out some samples. I also found some tailor-made cigarette butts on the way up to the shaft. That's about it. Billy told me that Charlie smokes tailor-mades, and he told me about Reid."

"So you figure what?" Hooley asked.

Slocum drank the rest of the coffee out of his cup. It had gotten lukewarm and left him wanting either a fresh, hot cup or a shot of whiskey. Either one would do. He put down the cup and continued his story.

"Well," he said, "I could be wrong. It could have happened any number of ways, I guess, but I figured that probably old Wade, while he was working for you, stumbled onto that mine shaft somehow. Then, instead of telling you about it, he went to some rich fellow, someone he knew who's got money enough to buy this place, and he told the rich fellow that he knew where there was a gold mine that the owner didn't even know about. The money man could buy the ranch and for his information, Wade would share in the profits from the mine.

"Whoever this money man is, he's also got Reid and Charlie on his payroll. Maybe some others. When you wouldn't even give Reid a price, they started running off your cattle. They burned your barn. The way I see it, that's all calculated to discourage you and get you to sell."

"It all makes perfect God damned sense to me," said Hooley, "and I'm convinced that you've got it figured exactly right. So where do we go from here?"

"You could announce to the whole world that

you've found a mine on your property," said Slocum, "and start mining it. With everything out in the open like that, there wouldn't be no game left for them to play. Your troubles would be over."

"And they'd have gotten away with murder, rustling, and barn burning," said Hooley, "and you'd still be on the lam. No. I won't do it that way."

"I didn't think you would," said Slocum, "but it's an option, and you have a right to consider it."

Hooley shook his head.

"No," he said. "Whatever we do, however we do it, I want to smoke the bastards out, and I want you to be able to ride out of here, or stay, as you will, a free and clear man."

"Well then," said Slocum, "tell me, who around here has got the kind of money it takes to buy a big spread?"

"That's easy," said Hooley. "There's only half a dozen besides myself. Malcolm MacDowel owns the Drownding Creek Bank. Sam Spotts has a cattle ranch south of here. Otis Johnson's a lawyer with a bundle of sound investments. Then there's Tom Coates, Burl Phares, and Matt Crocker."

"Crocker?" said Slocum.

"Yeah," said Hooley. "I know he doesn't give that impression, but that store you worked in is not all he owns around here. He's a pretty wealthy man."

"I'll be damned," said Slocum. "And he was only paying me—"

"John," said Jill. "You said that when you told the sheriff you didn't own a shotgun, he said you could easily have used one from Crocker's store."

"Yeah," said Slocum, musing. "He did say that."

"Well, so could Crocker have," said Billy. "Just as easy as you."

"That's right," said Slocum, "but we know that Charlie's in on this, too, and I seen two greeners in Bryce's office."

"If we move on Charlie or on Reid," said Hooley, "might we make their boss expose himself in some way?"

"We might just make him dig his hole that much deeper," said Slocum. "I don't know."

"What if we just grab one of them and bring him out here and beat the truth out of him?" said Jill.

"That's one way," said Slocum.

"I don't like it," said Hooley. "You can beat someone into saying anything you want him to say. Then get him on a witness stand, and he can deny it and tell how you got him to say it in the first place."

"At least we could get the name we want out of him," said Jill, "and then we'd know who it is we're dealing with."

"You're right there," said the old man, "but let's try to come up with something else before we go to that extreme."

"I've got an idea," said Slocum. "See what you think about this."

Billy Hooley rode into Drownding Creek and hitched his horse to the rail in front of Applegate's Palace. He stood for a moment on the board sidewalk and looked around to see who he could see. Then he turned and walked inside.

It was late in the afternoon. Most businesses in town were still open, but a few customers were already beginning to come into Applegate's. Billy went up to the bar and slapped a coin down in front of him. Frank the bartender looked up.

"Billy," he said, surprise in his voice and on his face. "What brings you in here?"

"What's wrong?" said Billy, a belligerent edge to his voice. "I'm old enough, and I've got money."

"Nothing's wrong, Billy," said Frank. "I'm just surprised to see you. That's all. You're welcome here. What can I do for you?"

"Give me a whiskey," said Billy.

"Sure."

Frank put a bottle and a glass on the bar in front of Billy and took the coin. Billy poured himself a shot and sipped from it.

"Leave the bottle," Billy said. He looked down the bar and saw a cowboy standing alone at the far end. "Hey, Muggs."

The cowboy turned his head and saw Billy standing there alone.

"Howdy, Billy," he said. "I ain't seen you for awhile. You doing all right?"

"Come on down here and let me buy you a drink, Muggs," said Billy.

It wasn't long before Billy's bottle was empty, and he bought another. He was pouring drinks around freely and talking loud. He was beginning to stagger just a bit and slur his words. Charlie walked in and noticed him immediately. The deputy stepped up to the bar a safe distance away from Billy and motioned for Frank.

"What can I do for you, Charlie?" Frank said.

"How long has Billy Hooley been here?" Charlie asked.

"That's his second bottle," said Frank.

"Is he all right?"

"He seemed a little bit testy," said Frank, "but he ain't caused no trouble."

"Well, okay," said the deputy. "I just wonder if his old man knows what he's up to."

Frank laughed.

"I doubt it," he said.

"Thanks," said Charlie, and he walked down the bar to step up beside Billy. "Howdy, Billy," he said. "How you doing?"

Billy turned his head slowly to look at Charlie. He squinted his eyes.

"Oh, Charlie," he said. "I'm doing just fine. Let me buy you a drink."

"Sure," said Charlie. "I'm off duty."

"Hey, Frank," Billy shouted. "Bring another glass."

"It's good to see you out and about," said Charlie. "You don't get in here very often."

He took out a tailor-made cigarette, struck a match on the bar, and lit his smoke. He started to put the box away, then he recalled something.

"Billy, boy," he said, "did you ever get yourself a box of these?"

Billy rolled his head toward Charlie and looked closely at the box in his hand.

"Oh," he said. "No. I ain't got around to it yet."

"Try one," said Charlie.

Billy took one of the tailor-mades and Charlie gave him a light. Just then Frank came back and put the glass in front of Charlie, and Billy, squinting as the cigarette smoke burned his eyes, poured the whiskey, putting about as much onto the bar as into the glass. Charlie lifted the glass and took a sip.

"Ah," he said. "That's good. You ought to come

into town more often, Billy boy."

"Hell," said Billy. "Papa keeps me too damn busy out there on the ranch, but all that's going to change now, I guess."

"How's that?" Charlie asked.

"Well," said Billy, "he's fixing to—Oh, shit. That reminds me. What time is it getting to be?"

Charlie pulled a watch out of his pocket, popped open the cover, and squinted at the face.

"About four," he said. "Why?"

"I got to go," said Billy, fumbling in his pocket for a piece of crumpled paper. "Papa sent me in to send off a telegram. If I don't get the damn thing off in time, he'll kill me."

He turned as if to leave, but his knees buckled, and he nearly fell.

"Shit," he said.

Charlie grabbed him by the shoulders to hold him up, turned him, and leaned him back against the bar.

"Hold on there, little buddy," he said. "Steady. You say you got a telegram to send?"

"Yeah," said Billy. "Papa will kick my ass if I don't get it off today. I got to go."

"Just hold on," said Charlie. "You won't never make it all the way down there, the shape you're in. Here. Steady yourself here. Let me have that note, and I'll go send the message for you."

Billy held the paper out toward Charlie, nearly dropping it on the floor. Charlie grabbed it and started reading.

"Does it say on here where it goes to?" he asked. "Is everything I need to know wrote down so that I can send it off for you?"

"Yeah," said Billy. "It's all there. Oh. Here."

He dug in his pocket again and brought out some coins, which he handed to Charlie.

"Be sure you get that off now," he said. "Papa—"

"Don't worry," said Charlie. He picked up the bottle and refilled Billy's glass. "You just relax now. I'll take care of everything."

12

Billy knew that he would have to hang around the saloon for a while longer in order to make the ruse work the way Slocum had planned. And he had done a good job so far with his part. He called some of his friends around him and poured more drinks for them, emptying the second bottle. Then he called for a third bottle and paid for it.

Playing his role carefully, he had managed to go through two bottles of whiskey without actually having drunk much more than a couple of shots, but with everyone else drinking from his bottles, and with the act he was putting on, all observers figured that he was roaring drunk. He continued to play the game.

• • •

Outside, across the street, in the shadows of the narrow space between two buildings, Jill sat on her horse and watched the front door of Applegate's. She saw Charlie come out, reading the paper he held in his hands. She watched as he looked up and down the street furtively and then started walking. But just as Slocum had expected, Charlie did not walk toward the telegraph office.

She almost lost sight of him, so she eased her horse just a little forward, just in time to see Charlie walk through the front door of Crocker's store. She fought off an impulse to follow him and actually see him in the act of showing the message to Crocker. *Crocker*, she thought. *The son of a bitch.* She turned her horse and rode out of town on a back street, headed for the ranch.

"I can't help but feel a little nervous here, Mr. Hooley," Slocum was saying. "I admit it's a hell of a lot more comfortable than that cabin on the hilltop, but I don't feel none too safe."

He was sitting in a large easy chair in the ample living room of Hooley's ranch house. His Appaloosa had been turned into the corral with the ranch remuda. Fortunately, old Hooley already had a couple of the spotted horses, and so it was not likely that anyone would pay particular attention to Slocum's horse in there. At least, that was what Hooley had said.

"Relax, Slocum," the old man said. "No one's going to find you here. Bryce has already been out here once to see me since your escape. Besides, he's not looking for you to be out here. He doesn't know anything about our connection, and he has no reason to suspect me or my kids. I've talked to Bryce. He's completely puzzled about your—disappearance."

"I know about that," said Slocum, "but what if one of your boys notices a new horse out there?"

"I'll tell them just that," said Hooley. "It's a new horse. I bought it for myself, and they're to leave it alone. That's all."

Slocum was still nervous. He had not been seen much riding around Drownding Creek, but his horse was a bit unusual, and one of the ranch hands might possibly recognize it as his and say something to Bryce or one of his deputies. When Hooley had invited him down to the ranch house, he had thought that it was probably not really a good idea, but he had been afraid that he was going stir crazy in the cabin, and so he had given in and accepted the invitation.

He decided to try to do as Hooley suggested and just relax. He had eaten a fine meal. Before they had left the cabin, Jill had cooked up those steaks she had promised him earlier. Billy had packed them up the hill in his saddlebags. And now Slocum was sitting in an overstuffed easy chair, enjoying a fine cigar and the best whiskey that money could buy. There was nothing cheap or stingy about Brett Hooley, and as far as Slocum was concerned, there was sure nothing wrong with his taste.

Mrs. Tilton was in Crocker's store when Charlie burst through the door. Charlie slowed himself down when he saw her and tried to cover up his hurry. The old woman was puttering around, looking at this and that, and Charlie wished that she would get her business done and get the hell out. Crocker was patiently standing behind the counter.

"What can I do for you, deputy?" he asked.

"Uh, them new six-guns you got in awhile back," said Charlie. "Can I look at one?"

"Sure thing," said Crocker, and he pulled a revolver out from under the counter and laid it in front of Charlie. Charlie picked it up and began to examine it minutely. Mrs. Tilton puttered some more. At last she laid her selections on the counter and Crocker totaled them up and wrote the amount in his book. Mrs. Tilton signed, took her packages, and left.

"I thought the old bitch would never leave," said Charlie.

"What's the matter with you?" Crocker asked. "She's a good customer."

Charlie shoved the rumpled paper at him.

"Read that," he said.

Crocker read out loud.

" 'To Anson Lewis,' " he said, " 'Abilene, Kansas. Your offer is acceptable. Come on down right away, and we will close the deal. Brett Hooley.' What the hell is this?"

"I got it off the Hooley kid," said Charlie. "He was in Applegate's, drunk as a skunk. That ain't like him, so I cozied up to him, you know? He grumbled something that sounded to me like he wouldn't be working the ranch for much longer, so I stuck around. Then he asked me what time it was. Said he had to get a message off by wire. His daddy had sent him into town to do that. Well, he was staggering drunk already, so I just kindly offered to send the wire for him."

"You didn't send it?" said Crocker.

"No," said Charlie. "Hell no. I ain't stupid. I got the message and his money, and I come straight here with it."

"Good," said Crocker. "Good. So my plan worked after all. We broke him down. But he's got a buyer from out of the territory. The old son of a bitch. We'll have to do something about that. Find Reid and send him over here. Right away."

"What are you going to do?" the deputy asked.

"Never mind that," said Crocker. "Just get Reid and hurry. Oh. Wait."

He pulled a pencil out of his pocket and wrote a message on a note pad. Then he tore off the top sheet and handed it to Charlie.

"After you find Reid, I want you to ride over to Stringtown and send these two messages."

Charlie took the note and read first a message to Anson Lewis in Abilene that said, "Forget it. The deal is off," and was signed, "Brett Hooley." The second message was addressed to Brett Hooley, Drownding Creek. It said simply, "I'm on the way," and was signed, "Anson Lewis."

"That's a long ride over to Stringtown," said Charlie. "I'm on duty in the morning."

"I don't give a shit about that," said Crocker. "You want a share of that gold, don't you?"

Jill was the first of the two young Hooleys to arrive back at the Hooley ranch house. She rode up fast, jumped from the saddle, and burst through the door into the living room. Slocum and Hooley were both already on their feet. They had heard her coming and looked out the window to make sure who it was.

"It's Crocker," she said. "Crocker's behind it all."

"Slow down, girl," said Slocum. "Tell us how you know."

Jill had to stand and draw in a few deep breaths before she could talk. Slocum handed her his glass, and she took a quick slug of whiskey. It made her cough. She handed the glass back.

"I was watching the front door of Applegate's," she said. "Charlie come out with the paper in his hands. He slowed down to read it. Then he went straight to Crocker's store. That's it."

Brett Hooley scowled deeply.

"Matt Crocker," he said. "I wouldn't have thought it of him. We've been friends—Well, we've known each other for years."

"Question is," said Slocum, "what do we do now that we know?"

"Let's wait for Billy," said Hooley. "Then we'll talk it out."

"Well, I hope he hurries," said Jill.

"You just abandoned that horse you rode," said Hooley, "and you rode him pretty hard. Get on out there and take care of him."

"All right," said Jill, and she flounced out the door. She took the reins to lead the horse toward the corral just as Billy rode up.

"Did you see him?" he asked. "Did you see Charlie?"

"I seen him all right," said Jill.

"Where'd he go?"

"Straight to Crocker."

"Crocker," said Billy. "Be damned."

He swung down to the ground and started for the porch, but his sister stopped him.

"Papa said we'll all talk it out," she said, "but he

sent me out here to take care of this horse. We might as well take care of both of them before we go back inside."

At last the four were all back together. Billy was excited and anxious to tell his tale.

"Everybody in Applegate's thought I was drunk as a skunk," he said. "I really put on a show. Hell, I ought to have gone on the stage. I just might do it yet."

"Cut out the bullshit, Billy," said Jill, "and get to the important part."

"I wish you wouldn't talk like that," said Hooley. "It doesn't become a young lady."

Jill bit her tongue and repressed an impulse to tell her father what she thought of both his wishes and young ladies.

"Well," said Billy, "I was just buying drinks around and playing drunk and waiting to see if either Charlie or Reid would come in, and sure enough, Charlie showed up. When he seen what I was up to, he sidled up to me and started talking. I waited a little while, and then I acted all in a hurry because I just realized how late it was and I needed to get down to the telegraph office, I said. I staggered a little, and old Charlie said that I wasn't in no shape to make it all the way down there, and he would do it for me. So I give him the note and some money, and he took off. That's about it."

"So Charlie promised to send the message," said Hooley, "but instead he took it straight to Crocker."

"That's right," said Jill. "I watched him come out of Applegate's, read the note, and hustle right over to Crocker's store."

"So where do we go from here?" said Slocum. "We still got nothing to take to court."

"In the old days," said Hooley, "I didn't need courts or sheriffs or anything else. We didn't have any. I took care of things myself. Me and my ranch hands. Seems to me that it's time to rely on my boys again."

"What about Bryce?" asked Slocum.

"We'll test our sheriff, too," said Hooley, "but we'll have the boys behind us just in case. First thing in the morning, Billy, get the boys all up here to the house. We'll tell them the whole story. Then we'll send someone in to fetch Bryce out here for a talk."

"Yes, sir," said Billy.

Hooley looked at Slocum as if to ask him what he thought of the plan.

"It's against my better judgment," Slocum said, "but I ain't got another idea, so I reckon I'll go along."

"Good," said Hooley. "Then I suggest we all turn in for the night. We'll have a big day tomorrow, and it'll start early. Jill, would you be good enough to show Mr. Slocum the guest room?"

"Sure," she said.

"Good night," said Hooley.

As soon as the old man had turned his back and was headed up the stairs, Jill looked at Slocum with a winsome smile.

"You ready to go to bed, Mr. Slocum?" she asked.

Slocum was keenly aware of the presence of Billy in the room, and he tried to act as if he had not noticed Jill's expression or tone of voice.

"Sure," he said. "I'm ready to turn in."

"Come on, then," said Jill. "I'll show you your room."

"Good night, Slocum," said Billy. "See you in the morning."

"Yeah," said Slocum. "See you."

He followed Jill to a door at the back of the big living room. She opened it and stepped aside, and Slocum went on through the door.

"I'll see you later," Jill whispered, and then she closed the door and left him alone.

13

Well, Slocum thought, *things are sure as hell looking up.* He had gone from a jail cell to the cabin on the hill, and then from the cabin to this finely furnished bedroom in a luxurious ranch house. His lifestyle was changing rapidly and always for the better. Yes indeed. Things were looking up.

A lamp was burning low on a table just inside the door. He turned up the flame to look over the furnishings of the room. A large, straight chair with padded seat and back was standing just beside the table, and, in addition to the lamp, the table held a bottle of good whiskey and a glass. There was also a box of cigars, a tin of matches, and a large cut-glass ashtray.

A matching table stood against the wall on the

other side of the door. On it were a pitcher of water, a basin, and a stack of towels. In the middle of the opposite wall was a large window, covered with a white curtain trimmed with lace, and just beside it a large, ornate wardrobe stood against the wall.

Slocum poured himself a drink from the bottle, picked up the glass, and turned to look at the rest of the room. The bed was huge and covered with a thick quilt. At its head were two large, fluffy pillows. He sat down in the chair beside the table and sipped his whiskey. Surroundings like this, he told himself, could make a man relax too much. Get him off his guard. He would have to be careful and not let that happen.

He reminded himself that he could easily find himself back in the Drownding Creek jail—or worse. He was, after all, still a fugitive from justice, however unjust that might be. He had been arrested and accused of murder, and in addition to that original charge, he was now also wanted for breaking jail and possibly for assaulting an officer of the law.

Of course, he hadn't actually done the assaulting, the Hooley kids had done that, but it had all been done on his behalf, and he was sure that he would be charged along with them, if the law ever got its hands on him again.

He chuckled at himself for thinking of Jill as one of the Hooley "kids," considering the time he'd had with her in the cabin, and the time he might have with her again right under her father's own roof. He wondered if he should feel guilty for that, but he decided not. True, she was young, but she was a grown woman, of legal age—at least, he thought she was.

Anyhow, he thought, pulling his mind back to the

analysis of his current situation, on top of all that other stuff, here he was living in the lap of luxury only a short ride from the sheriff's office in Drownding Creek. He didn't know whether to feel cocky or stupid about that simple fact, so he sipped some whiskey and enjoyed the feeling of it burning its way down his throat. Old Brett Hooley sure knew how to spend his money. Slocum had to hand it to him for that.

He took the rest of the whiskey in his glass with one swallow, put the glass back down on the table, and stood up. He took off his hat and hung it on a peg on the wall, removed his gun belt and put that on a bedside table where it would be within easy reach from his position in bed, then he undressed. Moving back across the room, he tossed his clothes on the chair, and then turned out the lamp.

The darkness of the room surprised him, and he stood there for a moment, allowing his eyes to adjust to the change. Then he made his way over to the bed. He was about to crawl under the bed covers when he hesitated, thinking again about Jill's last words to him.

He pulled off his underwear, dropping it to the floor, and climbed into bed naked, wearing nothing but a smile of anticipation on his face. If she did manage to sneak into the room later, as she had indicated she would, he would be ready for her.

He was tired and sleepy, but in spite of that, he lay awake for a while, anticipating her arrival. Recalling the pleasures of his previous tryst with her was enough to keep him awake for a time. But the big bed was wonderfully comfortable, and the covers were warm and cozy, and at last, in spite of it all, he dropped off to sleep.

She came into his dreams. She was kissing him on his mouth, his cheeks, his neck. Her hands roamed all over his body, and his rod stood up straight, making a tent of the quilt that covered him.

He could not see her for the darkness, but he knew that she was there. He knew it because he could feel her hands creeping along the insides of his legs, inching their way slowly upward.

And then he realized that he was actually awake again and was no longer dreaming, and the feel of her hands on his legs was real. He raised his head to look toward the foot of the bed, and in the darkness, he could not see clearly, but he could see the lump in the quilt where she had crawled in from the foot of the bed. She was actually there, between his legs, completely hidden under the covers. Slocum was suddenly wide awake.

She must have come quietly into the room, undressed, lifted the covers up from the foot of the bed, and crawled in under them, snuggling in between his legs, all while he slept. He recalled his earlier admonition to himself to remain alert in these surroundings, but the thought went quickly away again, for now she had a hand on each leg and was working her way up. And his hard-on was real, too. It was not just a dream. He could feel it down there, swollen and tight and standing up in anticipation of the joys to come.

Her hands were on the insides of his thighs, slowly stroking. He spread his legs a little to give her more room down there, and just then her fingers encircled his cock and balls and held them tight, and his anxious cock began to buck and jump. She grabbed it with one hand and squeezed it tight, holding it still. It pulsed and throbbed, still trying to buck, and then she flicked its head with the tip of her tongue.

Slocum's hips humped involuntarily, and she licked it again, this time more slowly and more fully, leaving it wet with her saliva. Then she pumped it with her hand, and he started humping rhythmically, fucking her hand, and after a few strokes, she took it into her mouth, and he continued fucking. He was fucking her face. He could feel her forehead and her nose against his belly, and her lips clamped around the base of his cock, and he wondered where it had all gone. Where was she putting it? Still he fucked.

It was getting warm under the heavy quilt, and Slocum tossed it back as far as he could, revealing most of his own body and about half of Jill's. His eyes had adjusted by then to the darkness of the room, and he could see her there, her head moving up and down along the shaft of his cock. He reached down with both hands and ran his fingers through her hair.

He gently pulled her toward his head, and she allowed the cock to slip out from between her tight lips. When it came free, it slapped against his belly, and she crawled slowly up until her face was just over his, and she lowered her face to kiss him on the mouth with open lips and probing tongue.

At the same time, she reached down to clutch his wet cock, and she lifted it and poked its head between her waiting cunt lips, and they were wet and slick. He went in easily, and she pressed down, taking it all. She pulled her face away from his and sat up.

She was on her knees, with him between her legs. He felt her weight pressing down against his crotch and hips, and then she started to rock slowly back and forth, and she moaned low with the pleasure of the motion of his cock inside her.

Then her moaning took on more urgency, almost a desperation, and her rocking was faster and faster, becoming a furious and violent thrusting of her hips. He could feel the backs of her upper thighs and the cheeks of her smooth, round ass sliding rapidly back and forth against him, lubricated by the combined sweat of their two bodies. And he could feel the juices from inside her oozing out and soaking his crotch and his balls.

Then she came. She stopped her thrusts, pressing hard against him. The fingers of both her hands dug into the muscles of his chest. She arched her back and threw back her head, moaning low through clenched teeth to suppress the primal scream that wanted to come out of her lungs.

Then she relaxed, breathing fast and deep, and she lowered her head and looked at him and smiled, and the expression on her face was one of total and complete pleasure. She started to move again, slowly, and slowly she built up speed, and then she came again. And again. And again.

At last she relaxed completely, falling forward to lie against him, and she covered his face with wet kisses, then lay still, breathing quietly, content.

"How many times was that?" he asked her, whispering in her ear.

"Oh," she said. "I don't know. A dozen at least. It's your turn now."

He wrapped his arms around her and, holding her tight, rolled to his left. On top of her then, her legs clamped around his waist, he drove hard into her.

Oh," she said. "Oh. Oh. Oh."

He drove harder and faster, trying to push deeper with each thrust, jarring her whole body as his pelvis slammed against hers. Her breasts bounced with each new impact. Her head lay to one side. Her eyes were closed. Her mouth was open wide, breathing deeply between the moans and groans.

He felt the pressure building until he knew that it would hold no longer. At last he came with a mighty surge. One gush followed another, until her insides were flooded, and the thick, rich semen, mingled with her own juices, ran out and puddled on the sheets between her legs.

Slocum relaxed, letting his entire weight press down on top of her for a moment. She squeezed him a few times with the walls of her cunt, a wonderful, milking kind of stroke. Finally, he pulled out of her and rolled over onto his back.

She left the bed, but she was back in a moment with a dampened towel, and she began to wash him off. He went to sleep while that was going on. It was a deep sleep, a restful sleep, the best and most satisfying sleep he had enjoyed for some time.

When Slocum next opened his eyes, the room was light, not bright, but lit with early morning light.

He turned his head to see Jill still beside him, naked, in his bed. He felt a sudden panic. Old
Hooley was the type to be up and about early in
the morning.

Jill was sleeping soundly, just as Slocum had slept,
and he hated to do it, but he knew that he must. It
might already be too late. He put a hand on her shoulder and shook her gently. It didn't work. He shook
more vigorously, and she smiled and rolled over. He
shook her once again.

"Jill," he whispered harshly. "Jill. Wake up. It's
daylight."

She moaned softly and rolled her head toward
him.

"What?" she said.

"Wake up."

She opened her eyes and saw that it was light.

"Oh no," she said.

"You've got to get out of here," he said.

She jumped out of the bed, found her clothes
where she had left them on the floor, and pulled
them on as quickly as she could. She moved quickly
back to the bed, bent over and gave Slocum a kiss
on the cheek, and pulled the covers up close under
his chin.

"Close your eyes," she whispered.

Then she walked boldy to the door, opened it,
and stepped out. As she closed the bedroom door
behind her, Brett Hooley stopped on the third step
from the bottom of the stairway. He turned his
head and looked at his daughter standing there
just outside the door of the bedroom in which
John Slocum was their guest. Hooley looked as if
he wanted to say something. He started to open

his mouth, but Jill beat him to the punch.

"Just checking on our guest," she said. "Hell. He's still sound asleep. You reckon we ought to start breakfast or what?"

14

When Slocum finally came out of the bedroom dressed and more or less prepared to face the day, he found the entire Hooley family just ready to sit down to breakfast, and he fancied that he received a sharp glance of disapproval from old Brett, but the old man didn't actually say anything, and Slocum decided that it was probably just his imagination or his guilty conscience or something, rather than anything real in Hooley's expression.

"Grab a chair, Slocum," said Billy, a big, friendly smile on his face. "You're just in time. It's all hot and fresh."

"You slept away half the morning," said old Hooley, in a stern voice with a scowl on his face. "That's not your normal behavior, is it?"

"No, it ain't," said Slocum, "but nothing about my life's been normal lately."

He pulled out a chair and sat down, and so did the others, all but Jill. She brought out a coffeepot and poured coffee all around. Everything else was already on the table, but no one made a move until she had returned and taken her seat. Then she picked up a platter of fried eggs, scooped a couple off onto her plate, and handed the platter to her father.

It wasn't long before Slocum's plate, like all the others, was heaped with eggs, fried potatoes, biscuits, and a big steak. And as hungry as he was after his active night, Slocum knew that he would have at least a second plateful before he was satisfied.

"Good food," he said between bites.

Old Hooley muttered in response, and Billy said, "It sure is."

"Well, there's plenty more of everything where that came from," said Jill, "so eat all you want. I know you must be hungry."

Slocum read more meaning than her actual words into what she said, and he hoped that old Brett Hooley had not. He had an uneasy feeling that she was toying with him there in front of her father, and he wanted to admonish her to be more careful.

If the old man knew what had been going on, first in the cabin, and now under his own roof while he was upstairs asleep in his bed, there was no telling what he might do. He might turn Slocum in to the sheriff, or he might just blast him to eternity right there in his house. Either way, he'd get away with it, too, for Slocum was a wanted man. And either way, under the circumstances, Slocum wouldn't blame the man a bit. He wouldn't like it, of course, but he wouldn't blame old Hooley.

He cleaned his plate and heaped it up again with a second helping of everything, wondering all the time if Jill's father suspected the real reason he was so hungry this morning. Well, if it was to be a last meal, he'd make it a damn good one. He was still eating when everyone else had finished, but the others all still sat at the table with coffee.

"Billy," said old Hooley, breaking what was to Slocum a tense silence, "when you're finished with that cup, go on out and round up the boys. Have them gather up out here in front of the house."

"Right now?" Billy asked.

"Soon as you're done."

Billy gulped down the rest of his coffee, got up from the table, and hurried out the front door, pulling his hat down on his head. Jill finished her coffee a moment later and started clearing the table.

"John," she said, "did you have enough to eat?"

"Oh, yeah," said Slocum. "Probably a little too much. Thanks."

Jill disappeared into the kitchen with an armload of dishes.

"Well," said Hooley, "today's the day."

"Yeah," agreed Slocum. "I reckon so."

He wanted to say more, but he didn't. He wanted to think of a reason for Hooley to put off his plans, but he couldn't think of one. A part of him wanted to saddle up his horse and ride far away. Jill came back to the table with the coffeepot in her hand.

"Refill?" she asked.

Slocum nodded his head, for his mouth was full, and she poured him some coffee, then turned toward her father.

"Papa?" she asked.

"No more for me," he said.

She took the pot and Hooley's cup and saucer back into the kitchen. The table was cleared except for Slocum's place. He was still eating. Hooley stood up, and Slocum felt conspicuous left there alone.

"Take your time," said Hooley. "There's no big hurry."

He put on his jacket and hat and walked out the front door. Slocum finished eating, got up, and carried his dishes into the kitchen. As he put them down on the countertop, Jill turned and threw her arms around his neck.

"Here. Here," he said. "It's broad daylight, and everyone's up and around."

"But no one's in the house," she said.

He put his arms around her and held her close. She did feel good. He nuzzled her neck with his face, and he liked the smell of her. Then they heard the sound of the front door closing, and they released each other and stepped apart. She looked up into his face and smiled.

"That was real good," said Slocum. "Thank you."

"The breakfast?" said Jill.

"Well, yeah. That, too."

He walked back into the living room and found Billy waiting there.

"The crew's all outside," said Billy. "Papa wants us all out there, too."

Jill came out of the kitchen, and Slocum and the two young Hooleys went out the front door to join old Brett on the porch. They stood there, facing a crew of a dozen rough looking cowhands, and Slocum felt as though they were all staring directly at him.

"Listen up, boys," said Brett Hooley. "I've got some important things to tell you about. First thing I want to do is introduce this man here to you, and I'm going to trust to your loyalty to keep his presence here a secret just among us. We'll let it out later in our own way and our own time.

"Boys, this is John Slocum. Some of you may already know that Slocum was arrested in Drownding Creek by Sheriff Bryce and charged with the murder of Rolfe Wade, and he escaped from the jail. They're looking for him now. So technically speaking, I'm harboring a fugitive right here in my home."

Slocum thought, *He's harboring more in his home than he knows about.*

"But there's more to the story than that," Hooley continued. "In the first place, Slocum's not guilty of that murder. Never mind just now how I know that. Just trust me. I know it. In the second place, it was Jill and Billy here that busted him out of jail.

"Boys, there's a gold mine on this ranch. None of us knew about it until Slocum here found it the other day and told us. But Rolfe Wade had found it earlier, and he didn't tell me about it. He told Matt Crocker, and Crocker decided to try to buy me out."

At that point in the tale, Hooley paused to let the cowhands mutter to each other and take in the situation. They all knew about the recent troubles, of course, but this was the first that they had heard of Crocker being the one behind it and why.

"Crocker enlisted Basil Reid and Sheriff Bryce's

deputy, Charlie Goober," Hooley went on, "and along with Wade, they commenced to rustling cattle and doing other things to annoy us out here, all calculated to frustrate me into selling the place. Reid even came out to ask me for a selling price, but I ran him off.

"Then they must have had some kind of falling out among themselves, and one of them killed Wade, and they blamed it on Slocum. He was handy, because he'd had a fight with Wade just before that, and the whole town had seen it.

"Now if I was to bother telling you all just how we found all this out, we'd be out here all day. So once again, for now, just trust me. We may be about to have a showdown here, and it may come to shooting. I don't know, but I want you all to hang around close in case we need you. You got all that?"

"Yes sir, Mr. Hooley," said a cowboy in front of the crowd. "We'll be right here, and we're behind you all the way."

"Good," said Hooley. "Red."

"Yes sir?" said a man standing back behind the others.

"Catch up a horse and ride into town," said Hooley. "Find Bryce. Don't let on to him anything I've told you this morning. Just tell him I want to see him out here at the ranch. Tell him I want to see him alone and right away. Ride back with him if you can."

"Yes sir," said Red, and he turned to run toward the corral.

"Okay, boys," said Hooley. "Just relax now, and hang around close."

He turned to face Slocum.

"Well?" he said.

"Well," said Slocum, "I'm still not sure I like it a whole lot."

"Well, like it or not, it's done," said Hooley. "And you agreed to it last night."

"I did. That's a fact," said Slocum. "But it still ain't comfortable from where I'm standing. I'm the one that's wanted for murder, and now there's twelve more men that knows it and knows I'm here, and you've got the sheriff coming out to see us."

"We can trust all these boys," said Hooley.

"Yeah," said Slocum. "Would you have said that when Wade was working for you?"

"One rotten apple doesn't spoil the barrel," Hooley said, "if you get rid of it soon enough."

Slocum watched Red come out of the corral and ride off in the direction of Drownding Creek. Then he turned and walked back into the house.

He thought about having a drink, but he decided that it was much too early in the day, and he needed to stay alert. He was nervous about the approaching visit of Bryce. What if Bryce didn't buy their story? If he listened to the whole thing, and then still insisted on arresting Slocum and taking him back to jail, what would Hooley do? Would the old man drive the sheriff off his property and take a chance on having the law come down on him? Would he cave in and let Bryce take Slocum?

He didn't really think that Hooley would do that, for if he did, Slocum could tell the sheriff who it was that broke him out of jail. Still, it felt chancy. He hefted the Colt on his hip and paced across the room a time or two, then sat down in an easy chair facing the front door. Jill came in from the porch.

"Don't worry about the sheriff, John," she said. "We won't let him take you."

"Are you a mind reader, too?" he asked.

"I heard what you said to Papa," she said. "Besides, I can see it in you. You're nervous."

He lifted his hands up off the big arms of the easy chair and spread them wide in a casual gesture.

"Look at me," he said. "I'm relaxed."

"Okay," she said. "You want a smoke?"

"Yeah," he said. "Thanks."

She brought him a cigar and a wooden match. She sat down on one arm of the chair and slipped the cigar between his lips. Then she struck the match on the underside of the table that stood beside the chair and held the flame to the cigar's end. Slocum puffed until he had the cigar going good. Jill held the burning match up between their two faces, pursed her lips and blew out the flame.

"Thanks," he said.

"When this is over, John," she said, "will you be moving on?"

"That's been my plan all along," he said.

"I wish you'd stay," she said, "but I won't try to hold you. I guess I always knew that you'd be leaving. I'll miss you, though."

"Jill," he said, "I—"

"No," she said, putting two fingers to his lips to shush him. "Don't tell me anything that you don't mean."

"I won't lie to you," he said. He puffed on the cigar, and the rising smoke hovered over his head. "If any woman was to ever tempt me to settle down, it would be you. But I've tried it before, and I just ain't the settling kind."

"Okay," she said, and she smiled. "I'll accept that, and I'll believe it. Anything I can get for you?"

"No, thanks," he said. "I'm doing just fine."

15

Basil Reid rode toward the Hooley ranch house. When he saw all the cowhands lounging around, he hauled back on his horse's reins. He sat there a moment, as if unsure of what to do. Then he rode ahead. Stopping in front of the porch at last, he looked at Brett Hooley standing there.

"Mr. Hooley," he said.

"Why am I not surprised to see you here?" said Hooley.

"Huh?" said Reid. "I don't know."

"Well then," said Hooley, "suppose you tell me what you want."

"I heard in town that you was fixing to sell your place," said Reid. "Someone from out of the territory. Well, that's what I heard. If you'll just tell me how much you want for it, I got a interested buyer right here. Local. Get the deal closed a whole lot faster."

"Who's your buyer?" Hooley asked.

"I, uh, I can't say just yet," said Reid.

Hooley stepped off the porch, walking toward Reid.

"Who is it?" he demanded.

Reid started to back his horse, but he found himself suddenly surrounded by cowboys. Hooley reached up and pulled him from the saddle.

"You talk to me, you little son of a bitch," the old man said, "or you'll by God wish you had."

"Boss," said a cowboy.

"What?" Hooley snapped.

"Red's coming back. Looks like he's got the sheriff with him."

Hooley flung Reid back against his horse.

"Get out of here, you little chickenshit," he said.

Reid mounted quickly, turned his horse, and rode away. Hooley stood watching him go and waiting for the arrival of the other two riders.

Inside the house, Jill was standing by the window, looking out, when Bryce and Red came riding toward the ranch house side by side. Slocum still sat in the easy chair. His cigar was long gone. He was just sitting there, waiting. Hooley was out on the porch with Billy. Some of the cowhands were lounging about on or near the porch. Some others were hanging around the corral not far away.

"Here they come," said Jill. "Bryce and Red."

"No deputies?" said Slocum.

"No," said Jill. "Bryce came alone, just like Papa asked him to."

Slocum stood and hefted his Colt. Then he walked to the door and opened it to step out onto the porch. Hooley turned to see who it was coming out.

"Stay inside, Slocum," he said.

Slocum backed up and closed the door. He wasn't sure why, but he wasn't going to argue. He guessed that the old man knew what he was doing. He walked back across the room to the chair he'd been sitting in, but he didn't sit. He stood there, watching the front door.

Outside, Bryce was keenly aware of the dozen armed cowhands lounging around the premises, all watching him as he rode up to the ranch house. He had known that something was up when Red had told him that Hooley wanted to see him alone. But Brett Hooley was one of the wealthiest and most highly respected men in the territory, and so Bryce hadn't argued. He figured that old Hooley must have his reasons.

Seeing all the cowboys like that, armed and not out working, Bryce wondered if maybe he had made a mistake riding out alone with Red. The two riders moved slowly up to the porch and halted their mounts. Bryce looked at Hooley standing there.

"Hello, Bryce," said Hooley. "Thanks for coming out."

"What's this all about, Brett?" asked the sheriff.

"Climb down and come in the house," said Hooley. "I'll tell you all about it. Red, take care of the sheriff's horse, will you?"

"Yes sir," said Red.

Both riders dismounted, and Red took the reins of both horses and led them toward the corral, as Bryce stepped up onto the porch. Hooley opened the front door and stepped aside for Bryce to lead the way. He and Billy followed.

When Bryce stepped inside the living room, he found himself facing Slocum across the room. He knew that Hooley had not captured the fugitive, for Slocum was wearing his gun. Jill was standing in the doorway to the kitchen, not far to Slocum's right, and Billy and Brett Hooley were right behind Bryce, and they were both armed. In spite of all that, instinctively, Bryce's right hand went for the revolver at his side.

"I wouldn't do that, Bryce," said Hooley. "In fact, if I was you, I'd take off that gun belt and hold it back over my left shoulder. Real easy."

"What the hell is going on here?" said Bryce.

Hooley thumbed back the hammer of his own revolver, and Bryce heard the unmistakable click behind his back.

"The gun belt," said Hooley.

Bryce unfastened the buckle and held the rig back over his left shoulder.

"Get it, Billy," said Hooley, and Billy stepped up behind Bryce to take the belt and gun. "Now, let's all go on in and take a chair," said Hooley, "and we can talk this whole thing over nice and quiet."

"It had better be good," said Bryce. "Otherwise, I've got you for harboring a fugitive and for interfering with an officer of the law."

"Sit down, Bryce," said Hooley, and Bryce sat in a chair facing Slocum. Hooley took one to Bryce's right, and Billy sat off to the sheriff's left, Jill moved on into the room and sat at the table.

"What's that fugitive doing here in your house," said Bryce, "and armed, too?"

"You just shut up and listen," said Hooley. "When I'm done, I think all your questions will have been answered, and then I'll want to hear what you have to say."

"All right," said Bryce. "Let's hear it."

"First off," said Hooley, "Matthew Crocker, Basil Reid, and your deputy, Charlie Goober, are in cahoots trying to drive me off my ranch."

"Oh, come on," said Bryce.

"Shut up and hear me out," said Hooley. "Rolfe Wade was in on it with them, but they had a falling out among thieves and killed him."

"Not Slocum, huh?" said Bryce, a skeptical sneer on his face.

"Not Slocum," said Hooley. "Here's what happened. Awhile back, while he was still working for me, Wade stumbled onto an old gold mine on my property. He didn't tell me. He went to Crocker. Crocker enlisted the help of Charlie and Reid. When they found out that I wasn't interested in selling at any price, they started stealing my cattle. More recently, they burned down my barn."

"And Slocum here?" asked Bryce. "What's he got to do with it?"

"Not a damn thing," said Hooley. "When Crocker and the others killed Wade, Slocum just happened to be handy for you to blame it on. That's all. It was their good luck and his bad luck. Nothing more."

"It's a good story," said Bryce. "What proof have you got?"

"You remember I told you that someone had been

nosing around in that pass over there?" said Hooley.
"Drove a wagon in?"

"I remember," said Bryce.

"Tell him, Slocum," said Hooley.

"I rode over there and found the tracks," said Slocum. "I nosed around to see if I could find a reason
for them to be in there. That's when I found the mine
up on the hillside. About halfway up on a little ledge,
I found the butts of some tailor-made cigarettes."

"When I asked Charlie where he got his," said
Billy, "he said that he had them ordered just for him."

"Sounds like old Charlie's been nosing around my
gold mine, doesn't it?" said Hooley.

Bryce scratched his head.

"Well," he said.

"Reid asked me for my selling price," said Hooley,
interrupting Bryce. "He's got no money. He had to
be asking for someone else. We decided to find out
who it is. Slocum thought this one up. I had Billy go
into town and act like he was getting drunk. When
Charlie spotted him and got friendly, Billy said he
had to go send a wire for me. Charlie offered to do
it for him. He took the note and read it. It was a fake.
It read like I was accepting a man's offer to buy my
ranch."

"Charlie didn't take it to the telegraph office," said
Jill. "He took it straight to Crocker. I seen him."

Bryce stood up, scratching the side of his head.

"And just now," said Hooley, "Reid came back to
try again."

"Yeah," said Bryce. "I saw him riding out. It does
seem to all fall into place. Still, you've got no proof
of anything. No real proof of who's been stealing
your cattle. No proof of who burned your barn. No

proof of who killed Wade. For that matter, you've got no proof that Slocum didn't do it."

"But you said you arrested me because you didn't know of anyone else who had a reason to want to kill Wade," said Slocum. "Gold is a pretty damn good reason, it seems to me."

"I have to agree with that," said Bryce. "I guess I really don't have enough cause to hold you for anything, Slocum. Except for breaking jail, and I guess under the circumstances I could let that one slide. By the way, how did you manage that?"

All three Hooleys looked at Slocum, waiting to see what he would say.

"Sheriff," he said, "I don't rightly remember just how that happened."

"Well, never mind about that for now," said Bryce. "When I get back to the office, I'll clear your name up. Then I'll get hold of Charlie and ask him some tough questions."

"Sheriff," said Slocum, "why don't you hold up on clearing my name." He could hardly believe he was hearing himself say it. Still, he went on. "We don't want to spook old Crocker and them guys just yet, do we? Let them think they're still in the clear over that killing, for awhile longer anyhow. You knowing I'm clear is enough for me for now."

"All right," said Bryce. "You might be right."

He put his hat on and walked to the door.

"Can I have my gun back now?" he asked.

"Oh, sure," said Hooley, and Billy jumped up to run over to Bryce and hand him the rig. "I'm sorry we had to do you that way, but we had to get you to sit still long enough to hear the story."

"Forget it, Brett," Bryce said, as he buckled the

gun belt back around his waist. "I'll be in touch."

Just then there was a loud knock on the door. Bryce stepped out of the way as Hooley yelled.

"What is it?"

The door opened and Red poked in his head.

"Man just brought this wire out from town, boss," he said.

Hooley rushed over to the door and took the message from Red. He looked it over quickly, then handed it to Bryce.

"What do you make of this?" he said.

Bryce read aloud.

" 'I'm on the way. Anson Lewis.' "

"Ha," shouted Hooley. "Have we got them or not?"

"What do you mean?" Bryce asked.

"There is no Anson Lewis," said Hooley. "I made him up. There's no way he could have answered my wire, the wire that Charlie supposedly sent. There is no Anson Lewis."

He jerked the paper back out of Bryce's hand and tucked it into his pocket. Bryce touched the brim of his hat.

"Like I said, I'll be in touch."

Hooley, Billy, Slocum, and Jill followed Bryce out onto the porch, and Hooley sent Red running for Bryce's horse. In a few minutes, Bryce was riding back toward town.

"What do we do now, Papa?" Billy asked.

"We sit tight," said Hooley. "We don't know what Bryce will do when he gets back to town. Don't know what he might set off."

"That bunch of cows up in the north pasture really needs to be moved," said Billy.

Hooley heaved a heavy sigh.

"You think six hands can take care of them?" he asked.

"Well," said Billy, "yeah. I guess so."

"Then send six out to do that job and leave the other six here," the old man said. "Right now, we can't be too careful."

Billy walked over to the edge of the porch to talk to Red, and Hooley turned to Slocum.

"What do you think?" he asked.

Slocum shook his head.

"I don't know," he said. "How well do you know Bryce?"

"Before all this happened," said Hooley, "I'd have said I know him as well as I know my own children. I never would have expected my children to break a man out of jail, and I thought that I knew Matt Crocker."

"What would you have said before about Bryce?"

"I'd have trusted him with my life."

"Well," said Slocum, "I ain't never trusted lawmen very much, but Bryce seems honest. Let's hope your original opinion was right."

When Bryce turned off the lane that ran up to the Hooley ranch house, he was riding along a tree-lined road that would eventually take him back into Drownding Creek. As he rode along, he mulled over the things that the Hooleys and Slocum had told him. They were all disturbing.

Of course, there was no proof against anyone, nothing, he thought, that would hold up in court. But then, he reminded himself, he hadn't really had anything on Slocum, either, and he had arrested him for murder. The circumstantial evidence that the Hooleys and Slocum had gathered against Crocker and his henchmen, if indeed they were that, was at least as good, probably better, than what he'd had against Slocum.

But Bryce had known Matt Crocker for years, considered him a friend. He didn't give a shit about Basil Reid one way or the other, but Charlie was his deputy, and he trusted Charlie. At least, he had trusted Charlie.

"Damn it," he said out loud. He did not like the way things were shaping up. But then, gold did strange things to people, even, he supposed, people like Matt Crocker and Charlie Goober.

He wondered just what he was going to do when he got back to town. He knew that he would do something. He had to. If Hooley's story was the truth, then as sheriff, he couldn't just let it ride. He would have to get to the bottom of it. Either that or resign.

For a brief moment, he thought about resigning and letting someone else worry about sorting out all the bullshit, but then he told himself that he had, after all, asked for this job, and it wouldn't do to quit just when the going got tough.

So the immediate question was just how to proceed. He could go directly to Crocker and confront him with the tale. What could Crocker say? He could say that Charlie had come into the store to buy something, and that he knew nothing of him promising to send a wire for Billy Hooley, and Bryce would be left standing there looking stupid.

He also had nothing on Reid. Reid had asked Hooley how much he wanted for the ranch, but that was all. But then, Reid had impressed Bryce as a little chickenshit, and Bryce thought that if he got

Reid alone, he could probably scare the truth out of him.

Charlie was a different matter. Charlie was tough, but Charlie also had several tough questions to answer. His cigarette butts had been found on the hillside leading up to the gold mine. At least, so Slocum said. And he had offered to send the wire for Billy and then gone to Crocker's store instead.

Bryce decided that he would have to confront Charlie with these questions. Charlie's response would tell him a lot about what to do next. Just then he rounded a curve in the road, and there in front of him, sitting on his horse directly in Bryce's path, was Charlie.

16

"I was worried about you, sheriff," said Charlie. "It ain't like you to ride off alone thataway, especially with that killer running loose."

"I rode out with Red," said Bryce.

"Yeah, but you're alone now," said Charlie. "Least-ways, you would be if I hadn't decided to follow along. How come old Hooley to want to see just you by yourself, anyhow?"

"Never mind that now," said Bryce. "Let's just get back to the office."

He urged his horse forward, and as he came alongside Charlie, the deputy turned his own mount around to ride along beside Bryce, but he allowed Bryce to get just a little ahead.

"What was on old Hooley's mind, anyhow?" Charlie asked again.

"Brett Hooley's an old friend of mine," said Bryce. "He just wanted a private conversation with me. That's all."

"I seen Basil Reid come riding down the road lickety split just a little while ago," said Charlie. "He said old Hooley was acting crazy. Had his whole crew armed and hanging around the house. Drove Reid off. Something's going on out there, and as your deputy, I ought to know about it."

"Charlie," said Bryce, "did you see Billy Hooley in Applegate's last evening?"

"Yeah. Sure. He was pretty drunk, too."

"Did you offer to send a wire for him?"

"Sure," said Charlie. "Nothing wrong with that, is there? I was just doing him a favor. He looked to me like he was about to fall down."

"Did you send it?"

"Well, sure I did," said Charlie. "I said I would, and I did."

"Brett Hooley got an answer to that wire this morning," said Bryce. "He showed it to me. 'I'm on the way. Anson Lewis.' That's what it said."

Charlie smiled.

"Well, see there. If I hadn't sent the first one, then how else would old Hooley have got his answer? See? I told you I done it. Just like I said I would. Is that what this was all about? Did that old son of a bitch say that I took Billy's money and didn't do what I said I would? Shit. I said I'd do it, and I did."

"Charlie," said Bryce, still riding slowly ahead, not looking back at Charlie, "you been my deputy quite a spell now. Number one deputy. Hell, boy, I've trusted you with my life. More than once. You know that."

"Yeah. I know that. Why, hell, sheriff, I'd do anything for you."

Bryce stopped his horse suddenly and turned in the saddle to look hard into Charlie's face.

"Charlie, you're lying to me," he said. "I didn't want to believe it of you, but you're lying. What did you do with that note you got from Billy Hooley? And where did that telegram from Anson Lewis come from? I want the truth, Charlie."

"Say," said Charlie, "I don't know what you're talking about. I took the God damned note down to the telegraph office just like I said I would, and I sent it off. I don't know nothing about no reply. That's the last time I do a favor for a drunk. Hell."

"Charlie," said Bryce.

"Damn kid couldn't hardly stand up. Can't hold his liquor. It ain't my fault."

"Charlie, shut up," Bryce snapped out loud. "Charlie, it was a trap, and you fell right into it."

"What? What are you talking about?"

"There ain't no Anson Lewis, Charlie," Bryce said. "Hooley made him up, and Billy wasn't drunk, either. He was faking."

Charlie stared at Bryce, for a moment unbelieving, taking in all this new information, slowly beginning to understand not only that he had been duped, but that he was caught for sure. He tried to think of something to say, some way to explain his actions to Bryce, some way out of the trap, but there was no way. There was nothing he could do to wriggle out of the snare.

He jerked his revolver and fired. Bryce wasn't prepared for that reaction from Charlie, and so he was a fraction of a second later than the deputy. Even so, both guns roared almost at once. Bryce fell backward out of his saddle with a splotch of red on the right side of his chest. At almost the same instant, Charlie felt the slug from Bryce's revolver tear at his ear, and he felt the hot sticky blood run down the side of his neck. He screamed in panic, and his horse reared in fright, dumping him onto the road. He landed hard, an instant after Bryce.

Even with a hole in his chest, Bryce rolled and scampered for cover off the side of the road. There wasn't much, just tall grass between the trees, but he managed to get himself behind a tree where he was fairly well covered. Gritting his teeth with the pain, he maneuvered himself into firing position, just in time to see Charlie dive into the weeds on the other side of the road. He sent a shot after him, but he knew that it was wasted almost as he fired it.

"Charlie," he called. "Charlie, you hear me?"

"I hear you."

"Come on out of there, Charlie. You can't get away with this, and you know it."

"I ain't going to let you put me in jail, Bryce," Charlie yelled. "Damn you. You shot my ear off. I'm bleeding like a stuck pig."

"Give it up, Charlie," said Bryce.

"I ain't going to. Come and get me."

Bryce wondered if Charlie knew just how much damage his shot had done. Neither man could move for fear the other would get off a good shot, and Charlie definitely had the advantage, for if Bryce didn't get attention soon, he would likely bleed to death. Bryce just hoped that Charlie didn't realize that. His only chance was to talk Charlie into surrendering.

"Charlie," he said. "Listen to me."

He felt himself getting weaker, and he tried not to let it show in his voice.

"Go to hell, Bryce. Go fuck yourself."

"Charlie, we know it all. The gold mine. You and Reid and Crocker. We know you killed Wade, too. It's all over. You might as well give up."

"If you know that I killed Wade," said Charlie, "then you know that I can't give myself up. I sure don't want to hang."

So it was all true, Bryce thought. He hadn't known that Charlie killed Wade, of course, but now he did. And Charlie hadn't denied any of the rest, either. He felt himself growing weaker. He couldn't let Charlie know that. He lifted his revolver and pointed it in the general direction of Charlie—or where he thought that Charlie was—and he fired. Charlie fired back with two quick panic shots.

Bryce lowered his hand. The revolver was getting awfully heavy. He laid his head against the tree trunk and closed his eyes. He was almost asleep, and then he realized that if he allowed himself to drift off, he would die. He would either die from his wound, or Charlie would come over and put another bullet in him to finish him off. He jerked his head up and forced his eyes to open wide. He tried to lift the revolver, but he could not. Then all the strength went out of his body at once, and he fell over on his side and knew no more.

Charlie lay on his belly in the tall weeds. He was afraid to move. He was greatly afraid of Bryce. The man had a powerful reputation as a gunfighting lawman that preceded his move to Drownding Creek, and Charlie had seen him in action a time or two.

He would never have dared to draw on Bryce except for the fact that he knew that Bryce would not be expecting it from him. That had given him a slight edge, the element of surprise, and even so, Bryce's shot had come only a split second after his own. He was God damned lucky, he knew, that Bryce had not killed or crippled him, had only mangled an ear. Charlie was amazed at the amount of blood that poured out of a torn ear.

He realized that Bryce had been quiet for some time now, and he wondered if the sheriff was up to something. Bryce was full of tricks. Charlie knew that well. He could be working his way around behind Charlie somehow, or he might just be playing possum, hoping to draw Charlie out into the open. *Well*, Charlie told himself, *it ain't going to work*.

"Bryce," he called. "Bryce. Where are you?"

There was no answer, and Charlie looked around, almost expecting the frightening form of Bryce to loom up on one side or the other. There was no movement, no noise. *How long will he play this game with me?* Charlie asked himself. *How damn long?* Then he had another thought.

Maybe I hit him. Maybe I hit him real good. Both shots had sounded almost together, and Bryce's shot had torn Charlie's ear. At that range, Bryce should have hit him dead center, but he had hit his ear. Something had thrown off his shot. *That's it*, he thought gleefully. *That's got to be it. I hit him. He's hurt. Maybe dead.* Not quite convinced, he lifted his head just a little to look across the road.

"Bryce? Bryce, you out there? Come on, Bryce,

talk to me. Talk to me if you're alive."

He lifted his head a little more, and when no shot came, he got to his hands and knees. He waited a little more, then slowly stood. Still no shot. He moved quickly behind a nearby tree and pressed himself against it. *If Bryce was alive over there*, he thought, *he'd have shot at me while I moved.*

He stepped out from behind the tree and began walking slowly across the road, holding his revolver ready, beads of sweat popping out on his forehead. He felt a throbbing on the side of his head from the torn and mangled ear. He stopped in the middle of the road, looking around, ready to shoot in any direction. All was silence.

He moved on, stepping off the road again into the tall weeds on the other side. He looked around. Where could Bryce have gone? He could have gone in any direction, behind any tree. He could be down low in the tall grass anywhere. He moved in farther. He had to know that Bryce was dead.

17

They heard the gunshots back at the ranch house, Hooley and Slocum and the others. Billy was already gone with the six cowhands, but Jill looked at her father and then at Slocum.

"Sounds like somewhere between here and town," said Hooley.

"Bryce?" Slocum asked.

Without another word, the three ran outside together.

"Get us some horses saddled," Hooley shouted, and Red and two other cowboys ran for the corral. Hooley shot Slocum a quick glance. "You sure you want to ride out of here?" he asked.

"Hell," said Slocum, "everything's out in the open now."

Soon the three were mounted.

"You want us to come along, Mr. Hooley?" Red asked.

Hooley was already riding, so he shouted back over his shoulder.

"Send a couple of boys, Red," he said, "but you and the rest stay here."

They rode hard down the lane and turned left on the road that led to Drownding Creek. The two Hooleys were galloping hard, until Slocum shouted to them.

"Slow it down," he said. "We don't want to ride right into the middle of something before we know what's going on."

They all slowed their pace then. Still, they rode anxiously and alert. There were no more shots. Hooley and Slocum glanced at one another. No words were exchanged. They weren't needed. Each man knew that the fight must be over, and someone was probably dead.

The old man pulled a Winchester out of the boot tied to the right side of his saddle and levered a shell into the chamber. Slocum touched the butt of the Colt at his side. Jill also pulled out a rifle. Two cowboys came riding up behind them just then, and as they caught up, they slowed their pace to match the others.

Charlie looked behind one tree and then another. He knew that Bryce was down somewhere, almost for sure hit bad, but he needed to make sure that the sheriff was dead, for the sheriff now knew it all. He was moving cautiously to his left when he heard the sound of the pounding hoofs of several riders. It had to be Hooley riders. He looked around a little more, quickly and not well, glancing back and forth toward the approaching new threat. When it sounded like they were almost on him, he abandoned his search and ran for his horse.

Just as the riders from the Hooley Ranch rounded a curve in the road, they saw a man on horseback vanishing in the direction of Drownding Creek, but the dust he kicked up obscured him from their sight. They rode slowly forward. A saddled horse was grazing on the side of the road.

"That's Bryce's horse," said Hooley.

"Someone must have bushwhacked him," Jill said.

Slocum swung down out of the saddle.

"Let's find him," he said.

They all dismounted and began a search of both sides of the road. It wasn't long before one of the cowboys shouted.

"Over here."

They crowded around Bryce where he lay on the ground, seemingly lifeless, in an enormous pool of blood.

"Is he dead?" asked one of the hands.

Hooley shoved his way through the small crowd and dropped to his knees. He got an arm under Bryce's head and lifted it, leaning forward until his face was close to the lawman's.

"He's alive," he said. "Just barely. Someone fetch a buckboard. Hurry."

A cowboy ran for his horse to obey the command.

"Joe, ride to Stringtown for Doc Bliss. Tell him to hurry," Hooley continued, and another cowhand took off like a shot.

"We got to try to stop this bleeding," said Hooley. "Judging from the looks, there ain't much blood left in him."

"Ain't there a doc in Drownding Creek?" Slocum asked.

"Doc Bliss is the closest we got," said Hooley.

Jill gathered up a handful of something mossy and knelt beside her father. She mashed the stuff onto the raw hole on the sheriff's chest.

"Check his back," she said.

Slocum helped Hooley raise Bryce forward, and there was another hole in the back, worse than the entry wound. Jill mashed some more of the stuff she had gathered on that wound.

"That should stop it," she said. "At least we won't have to dig for a bullet."

When the buckboard finally arrived, they loaded Bryce into it and drove back to the ranch house. Then they carried him inside and laid him in the bed in the guest room, the room that Slocum had been occupying. He was still unconscious, looking very pale and more dead than alive.

They stripped him of his boots, socks, trousers, and shirt and pulled the covers up over him. Jill wrapped him tightly in bandages, then got a wet towel and bathed his face and neck.

"I don't know what else I can do," she said. "If I try to wash the wounds, they might start to bleed again."

"You've done everything you can for now," said Hooley. "We'll just have to wait for the doc."

Hooley and Slocum went back into the living room

and sat down in easy chairs. Jill stayed by the bedside in the guest room.

"It must have been Charlie," said Hooley. "I can't imagine Matt Crocker in a gunfight, and Basil Reid's a chickenshit. It had to have been Charlie."

"Unless Crocker's got more of an army than we know about," said Slocum.

"I think we'd better brace ourselves for a fight," said the old man.

"Or else plan our own attack," said Slocum. "Either way, if I was you, I'd call the rest of them cowhands back in."

"That's a good idea," said Hooley. "I don't know why I let Billy talk me into sending them out in the first place."

He heaved himself up out of the chair and headed for the door.

"Likely 'cause you've got a cattle ranch to run here," said Slocum, "and we didn't have no way of knowing how this thing was going to break. Don't blame Billy."

Hooley opened the front door and yelled for Red, then told him to send someone out to bring all the hands back in. That left only four of the hands at the ranch house until Billy and the others got back. Hooley saw to it that the four were well armed and alert on the front porch of the house. Then he went back to his seat in the living room.

"I wonder why Charlie did that?" he said. "If it was Charlie."

"Only thing I can figure," said Slocum, "is that Bryce confronted him with some hard questions, like he said he was going to do."

"Out there on the road like that?"

"Maybe Charlie got worried when he seen Bryce ride out here alone," said Slocum. "Maybe he followed him and waited for him back there."

"Well, one thing's for sure," the old man said. "If that's what happened, Charlie's telling Crocker all about it right now, and they're planning their next move."

It was late that evening by the time Doc Bliss showed up. By then all the cowhands were back at the house and on guard, watching all possible avenues of approach. Counting Slocum and the two male Hooleys, there were fifteen men, and Jill was a fighter, too, so actually there were sixteen.

Bliss unwrapped the bandages and cleaned the wounds and put on fresh bandages. He left Jill with a supply of bandages, some ointments and powders, and detailed instructions.

"You did real well, young lady," he said. "Just follow my instructions and hope for the best. He might pull through. Then again, he might not."

"It's pretty late, Doc," said Hooley. "You're welcome to stay the night."

"Well," said Bliss, "that would allow me to keep an eye on our patient here during this critical time. I'll leave early in the morning—uh, after breakfast."

In the back room of Crocker's store, the room that Slocum had occupied during his clerking days, Crocker, Charlie Goober, and Basil Reid met in secret.

"I didn't have no choice," Charlie was saying. "If I'd have let him get me back in town, I'd be in jail now. I only had a second to make a decision, and I shot him. He knows everything. He told it to me right down the line. He knows that it's the three of us, and he knows that Wade was in on it, too, and that we killed Wade. He had us dead to rights."

"But he had just come from Hooley's place," said Crocker, "and likely that means that Hooley and his bunch know it all, too. So even with Bryce dead—"

"I ain't really positive he's dead," said Charlie. "I mean, I think he is. I know I shot him, but before I could find him, they come riding at me from Hooley's, and I had to get out of there."

"Damn," said Crocker.

"Oh shit," said Reid. "We're really in trouble now."

"Shut up," said Charlie.

"Both of you shut up and let me think," said Crocker. "Now, let's see. We have to assume that everyone out at Hooley's ranch knows the whole story. If Bryce is dead, you'll be sheriff."

"Acting sheriff," said Charlie, "until the next election."

"That's good enough," said Crocker. "As acting sheriff, you could declare the whole bunch out there to be outlaws, say they're in league with Slocum, and they killed the sheriff."

"Then what?" asked Charlie. "Just ride out there and arrest them? Me and George? They's a dozen cowhands out there with them, and I reckon they'll all fight for old Hooley. We wouldn't have a chance."

"Of course you would," said Crocker. "First, we spread the story all over town that Slocum's been hiding out at Hooley's, and that they killed Bryce. Then you raise a posse, a good-sized posse made up of good citizens. When you ride out to Hooley's with a posse of a dozen or twenty men, what do you think

Hooley will do? Surrender?"

"Hell no," said Charlie. "He'll fight."

"And then you'll wipe him out," said Crocker. "All of them. While you're at it, you'll find out whether or not Bryce is really dead. If he's not, finish him, too. With no one left alive to argue, who would question your actions as sheriff?"

"Well, no one, I guess," said Charlie. He pulled a tailor-made cigarette out of his pocket and lit it with a match from a tin. "It might work, at that."

"Of course it will work," said Crocker. "It has to work."

18

Matthew Crocker sent Charlie Goober and Basil Reid off into the night with plans to start telling the trumped-up tale and rounding up a posse first thing in the morning. It sounded like a good enough plan. That is, it sounded good enough to convince those two idiots, Crocker told himself.

Actually, he knew that there were several holes in the plan, but he didn't really care. For instance, how likely would it be that a posse of mostly good citizens would actually wipe out twelve hardworking cowboys, old man Hooley, his daughter, and their own wounded sheriff—if Bryce was not yet dead?

Sure, there would probably be a fight, for Charlie would start it, and some would likely wind up getting killed on both sides, but a wholesale massacre? It just wouldn't happen that way. There were bound to be some left to tell the tale, and the truth would eventually come out. Too bad, but that was the way it looked.

Nor was it likely that very many folks in the Drownding Creek area would believe anything ill of Brett Hooley. He was too much respected and too well liked. Hell, even Crocker liked him, but then, friends were one thing, and gold was gold, and Crocker had wanted Hooley's gold in a real bad way.

Crocker knew when he was licked. He knew when it was time to tuck his tail and run. He also knew that his time was running out. Even if Bryce was dead, Hooley knew the whole story now, and Hooley was going to do something about it. He might send for law from outside, a U.S. marshal or something, or he might simply resort to his old ways and come riding into town with his entire crew ready to take the law into his own hands. Crocker knew that Hooley was capable of doing just that. He had done it before.

Either way, as things had shaped up, Hooley would win in the end. In any direct confrontation, Hooley would win. Crocker's only chance of beating Hooley from the beginning had been by deception, and now that chance was gone. So Charlie Goober and Basil Reid would unknowingly buy Crocker a little more time. While Hooley and the others were fighting off the posse that Charlie would raise, Crocker would be clearing out.

He would have to take a loss. He knew that, for he owned property in and around Drownding Creek, and he couldn't take that with him. But he did have a substantial amount of cash, both in his own safe and in the bank, and it would be ample to get him well set up and started over in some other place.

It was a shame to have to leave behind the other property and all of Hooley's gold, but Crocker had gambled big and lost, and he accepted that. The thing to do was to get out with as much as he could, keeping himself alive and out of prison. He couldn't stand the thought of prison, and he sure wasn't ready to die.

He started that very night by emptying his safe into saddlebags. He would have to wait until morning for the bank to open to get his money out of there, but as soon as he had done that, and while the rest of the town and the Hooleys were occupied by the excitement of the posse, he would get a horse and ride out toward Stringtown. At Stringtown he would be able to catch a train. It didn't really matter to him which direction the train might be headed. He would catch the first one leaving town. By the time the fight was over and anyone started to wonder where he was, he would be long gone on his way to some place where he could start over again.

Breakfast was over at the Hooley ranch house, and Doc Bliss repeated his instructions to Jill before taking his leave. Bryce was still unconscious, his condition still uncertain. The twelve cowboys still watched and waited outside for any sign of trouble, and Slocum was still asking himself just why in hell he had stuck around for so damn long.

Jill had slept the night sitting up in a chair in the guest room in case Bryce should return to consciousness or indicate in any way that he needed some kind of attention. Doc Bliss had slept on the couch in the living room, and Slocum, sitting up in an easy chair. It had been a rough night for all.

With Doc Bliss gone on his way, Slocum and Hooley discussed their options. They talked about mounting up the whole crew and riding into Drownding Creek to have it out once and for all with Crocker and his bunch, however many of them there might be. They agreed that they could probably win that kind of fight.

In the end, however, they decided against that course. It would certainly make them appear to be the aggressors, and if there was any doubt in anyone's mind, such action just might sway their opinion to the other side, especially if Bryce failed to pull through to substantiate their story. They decided to tough it out at the ranch house and wait for Crocker to make the next move.

Walking toward the bank, Crocker noticed with satisfaction that Charlie Goober had already gathered a crowd out in front of the sheriff's office. George, the other deputy, was standing beside Charlie looking a bit puzzled by it all, and Basil Reid was right in front of the crowd agreeing with everything that Charlie said. Crocker hurried on into the bank.

He went straight to the teller's window and laid his saddlebags down on the counter.

"I'd like to make a withdrawal," he said.

Outside, Charlie was calling for attention, and the crowd quieted down.

"I've got some bad news to tell you," he said, "and then I've got some more news that might shock some of y'all, but it's got to be told. Sheriff Bryce was shot and killed out on the road yesterday."

The crowd murmured in shock and disbelief, and Charlie held up his hands for quiet.

"Now y'all know about Slocum, the escaped killer," he said. "Yesterday we got word that he was hiding out at Hooley's ranch. Bryce went out there to check on it. I wanted to go along with him, but he told me to stay in town. He said he could handle it.

"Well, it didn't seem right to me, so I followed along on the sly. I was watching the ranch house from a distance, and I seen a whole army of gunfighters out there guarding the house. After awhile I seen Bryce come back out of the house and start to ride away, and then I seen them shoot him in the back.

"Well, I guess that makes me the acting sheriff, and right now I need a posse. I need all the able-bodied men I can get. If you got a horse and a gun, go get them and come right back here. We're going to ride out to Hooley's and clean out that nest of killers and thieves."

"Are you sure about all this, Charlie?" asked a man near the front of the crowd. "I've known Brett Hooley for years, and I just can't believe this of him."

"I wouldn't have believed it, either," said Charlie, "I swear. I wouldn't, but I seen it with my own eyes. They shot poor old Bryce right out of the saddle. I'm sorry I can't show you the evidence, but if I'd have tried to ride in there and get him, or what was left of him, they'd have killed me, too."

The men in the crowd began to talk among themselves.

"What do you think?"

"Don't know why Charlie'd lie to us."

"He said Slocum's out there. Slocum killed Rolfe Wade, didn't he?"

"That's what Bryce arrested him for."

"And Slocum's out there at Hooley's."

"Well, I don't know about the rest of you boys, but I'm going home for my horse and gun."

"Yeah. Me, too."

"Old Hooley's men run me off from out there just the other day," said Reid. "Threatened to kill me."

Crocker came out of the bank, his saddlebags considerably heavier than before. He hesitated on the sidewalk, taking in the growing excitement of the crowd. Charlie noticed him across the street and caught his eye. Crocker smiled and gave Charlie an approving nod, then walked on.

Back in his store, Crocker loaded a Webley Bulldog pocket pistol and dropped it into his right-side coat pocket. He put a box of shells for the Webley into his left-side pocket. He tightened the straps on the saddlebags, picked up his hat and his greatcoat, and walked to the front door to look out on the street.

Men on horseback were already beginning to gather again in front of the sheriff's office. Crocker would wait until they rode out of town before making his own move. It shouldn't be much longer. Then he saw Mrs. Tilton walking toward the store, and he quickly turned over the sign in the window to read Closed.

Mrs. Tilton stopped and stared at the sign for a moment with her face pinched into an expression of both disbelief and disapproval. Then she moved on to the door and pulled it open, stepping boldly inside.

"I'm sorry, Mrs. Tilton," Crocker said, "but the store is closed today."

"Closed today?" she said. "Why would it be closed today? This is a regular workday, and I have some shopping to do."

"You see," he said, "I lost my clerk. Slocum, you know. And I haven't been able to find a replacement for him yet. I have other businesses besides this store, and I'm just not able to take care of everything myself. I'm sorry, Mrs. Tilton, but I really have to close up now. Please excuse me."

"You're here, aren't you?" she said. "I only need a few things."

Glancing out of the window, Crocker saw the posse start to ride. He didn't have time to count them, but he estimated that there were somewhere around twenty men. They should keep Hooley and his bunch occupied for awhile, but Crocker needed to get out while the getting was good.

"Mrs. Tilton," he said, "I really have to go, but I'll leave the door unlocked. Just help yourself to whatever you want."

"But I—"

He hurried out the door, leaving her standing there with her mouth open. She stared after him for a moment, closed her mouth, shrugged, and began poking around the store. Crocker walked at a brisk pace to the livery stable and went inside. Abner Jones heard him come in and looked up from where he was busy mucking out a stall.

"Mr. Crocker," he said, "what can I do for you?"

"I need to rent a horse, Ab," said Crocker. "Have you got a good one for me?"

"You want one that will run hard and fast or slow and steady?" Jones asked.

"Slow and steady will do for me," said Crocker. "Easy to handle and dependable."

"I'll saddle old Molly here for you then," said Jones. "She ain't too fast, but other than that, she's the best horse I've got."

"Old Molly will do just fine," said Crocker.

Jones got Molly ready and led her to Crocker by the reins.

"When you bringing her back?" he asked.

"Why, uh, tomorrow afternoon," said Crocker. "Is that all right?"

"Sure," said Jones. "I just like to know, that's all."

"Well, how much do I owe you?"

"Aw, you can pay me when you get back, Mr. Crocker," said Jones. "That'll be soon enough."

So Crocker mounted old Molly and rode out of Drownding Creek at a leisurely pace, headed for Stringtown, while Charlie and his posse rode hard on the road toward Hooley's ranch, ready for action.

Red was the first one to see them.

"Take cover, boys," he shouted. "Be ready for anything."

He ran to the front door of the ranch house to inform Hooley, but the old man had already heard. He was coming out the door.

"Bunch of riders coming, Mr. Hooley," said Charlie. "I'd guess about twenty."

Hooley stepped out onto the porch, a six-gun strapped around his ample waist and a rifle in his hand. Slocum stepped out to stand beside him, similarly armed. They were followed closely by Billy and Jill.

"Get back inside, Jill," said the old man. "There's going to be a fight almost for sure."

"I can shoot as good as any man here," Jill said.

"A gunfight's no place for a young lady," he snapped back at her.

"It ain't no place for an old man, either," she said.

The approaching posse was now close enough to recognize individual riders.

"That's Charlie, all right," said Billy. "Riding up front."

"Yeah," said Hooley. "George is with him and Basil Reid. The rest all look like good citizens to me."

"Charlie must have fed them all a fine line of bullshit," said Jill.

"Boys," shouted Hooley, "let's try not to kill any of those good citizens if we can help it. Nobody shoot until I give the word."

The posse turned the corner, riding onto the lane that would lead them up to the ranch house. In a few yards, Charlie called a halt. He stared ahead for a moment in silence. He hadn't quite anticipated this kind of reception.

"They sure enough look to be ready for a fight," George said.

"We got them outnumbered," said Charlie.

"Not by much," said Reid.

"Well," said Charlie, pulling out his revolver, "ain't no sense in putting it off no longer."

"Hadn't we ought to try to talk them into giving up before we start shooting?" George asked.

Charlie hesitated. He wanted no more talking. He

was ready for a fight. Besides, he needed to kill all of that Hooley crowd, but he did have a small army of good citizens at his back. He had to make things look right for them.

"Yeah. Sure," he said. "Why don't you ride on up there real slow-like and see if you can have a talk with them?"

19

As George rode slowly forward, Jill cranked a shell into the chamber of her Winchester and threw the rifle to her shoulder, taking a deadly bead on the deputy.

"Jill," snapped Hooley. "Don't shoot. He's riding up to talk."

"I'm just getting ready," she said, "in case I don't like what he has to say."

George stopped about twenty yards away from the porch and looked over the scene in front of him. The three Hooleys and Slocum were standing on the porch. Jill had a rifle to her shoulder, and it was aimed at George. The dozen cowhands who worked for Hooley were scattered to the right and left of the porch, many of them holding rifles at the ready. They were concealed behind barrels, wagons, bales of hay, anything there that might provide them with some cover.

If it came to a fight, George could see, it was going to be a tough one, and the posse could easily come out the loser. Again he wondered if Charlie really knew what the hell he was doing, but with Bryce gone, Charlie was the boss, at least for the time being.

"Mr. Hooley," he called out.

"I'm here," said Hooley.

"Can we talk this over before anyone gets hurt?"

"You're the ones who rode armed onto my property looking for a fight," said Hooley. "I'm not out to hurt anyone, but I will defend myself."

"Well, Mr. Hooley, sir," said George, "we ain't looking for a fight, either, but Charlie says that someone out here at your place killed the sheriff. What do you know about that?"

"It's a God damned lie," shouted Jill.

"Hush, Jill," said Hooley. "George, you listen to me now. Bryce is in the house. He's in bed in my guest room. He's been shot, all right, bad, but he's not dead. I've had the doc here from Stringtown to look at him, and we're doing the best we can for him."

"He's not dead?"

"No, sir, he's not," said Hooley. "You're welcome to come inside and see for yourself if you want to. Just you. If you want to do that, you have my word, no one will harm you."

George was puzzled. He didn't know what to do. He looked back over his shoulder toward Charlie and the posse. They were too far back and couldn't hear what was being said. Charlie had said that the

Hooleys had killed Bryce, and Hooley said that he was inside in bed, hurt. Someone was lying, and George wanted to know who. He had to make a decision on his own.

"You sure Bryce is in the house?" he asked.

"I'm sure," said Hooley.

"Alive?"

"The last time I looked."

"Well, who shot him then?"

"We don't know," said Hooley. "We found him on the road and brought him here."

"But we got a strong suspicion," said Slocum, "that the shooter is back there behind you leading that posse."

George wrinkled up his face in puzzlement.

"You mean Charlie?" he asked.

"Why else would he tell a lie that he seen someone here do the shooting?" Slocum said.

"Come on in, George," said Hooley. "Jill, lower that damned rifle."

Jill dropped the Winchester to her side, and George rode slowly toward the house. Close to the porch, he dismounted.

"What the hell's he doing?" Charlie said.

"Trying to talk them out of a fight," said a man behind him. "Seems like a good idea to me. Ain't you s'posed to try to arrest someone peaceful before you start shooting?"

Charlie could see the plan that had seemed so simple before falling apart right in front of him, and he couldn't afford to have it fail. There was too much at stake. The shooting had to start.

"No," he shouted. "They ain't talking. They've captured George. Come on."

He cocked his revolver, yelled, kicked his horse viciously in the sides, and rode hard toward the house. The others hesitated a moment, unsure, then rode after him. Still too far away to do any good, someone fired a shot.

On the porch on his way inside, George heard the commotion behind him and looked back to see the posse attacking the house. Frantically, he waved his arms.

"No," he shouted. "Wait."

More shots were fired, and Hooley pulled open the door.

"Get inside," he said. "That damned Charlie means to kill us all."

Slocum shoved first George and then Jill through the door, and Hooley quickly followed them inside. Then Slocum ran to his left and dropped down off the porch at that end, squatting down to take cover behind it. He took careful aim with his Winchester and sent a slug into Basil Reid's thigh. It must have gone all the way through, because the horse dropped. Basil screamed in pain, but he managed to fall free.

As soon as Slocum fired his shot, the cowboys all began firing. Two more horses fell, and a couple of the posse men were wounded. Under the withering fire, Charlie turned and led a desperate retreat back toward the main gate, a safe distance away.

"What do we do now, Charlie?" someone asked.

"That was stupid, Charlie," said another. "Hell, we

can't take them like that. They'll cut us to pieces. They've got good cover."

"We've got some wounded here," said another.

"I'm bleeding to death over here," said Reid.

"I ain't so sure they captured old George, anyhow," said another.

Inside the house, Jill took George straight to the guest room to see the sheriff. She told him quickly about Bryce's visit to the house and what they had talked about. Then she told him about hearing the gunshots just after Bryce had left the house, and riding out to find him beside the road.

"And he never told you who shot him?" George asked.

"He's been unconscious the whole time," Jill said. "He'd already lost a lot of blood by the time we found him out there. The doc said he might come out of it, and he might not."

George scratched his head in puzzlement.

"Damn," he said. "We got to figure out some way to stop Charlie and them."

"Maybe some of us can work our way around behind them," Charlie said.

"Hell," said one of the men. "That's as stupid as your first idea. That's all open country. They'd see us all the way."

"We've got to get these wounded men to town," said another man.

"I need every man here," said Charlie.

"Forget it," said another. "I'm going back to town. I've had enough of this shit."

"Me, too," said yet another. "Let's help these fellows."

By the time they had helped Reid and the other wounded men into saddles and mounted up to ride double with them, a few others decided to go back with them. Charlie looked around and saw that his twenty-man posse had shrunk to twelve.

"Hell," he said. "They've got us outnumbered now."

"What are we going to do, Charlie?"

"I don't know. I don't know. Let me think."

George still stared down at Bryce, wondering what to do. He wasn't used to thinking on his own. Bryce had always told him every move to make. He noticed that the firing had stopped outside, and he thought that he might be able to go back out there and ride over to the posse to tell them what he had found out. Charlie wouldn't like it, especially if Charlie had done what the Hooleys said he had done, but if George could get the others to listen to reason, he might at least be able to get the posse members to ride back into town. That wouldn't solve all the problems or answer all the questions, but it would buy a little time and prevent any unnecessary killing, at least for the time being. He had just turned to walk out of the room, when he heard a weak voice behind him.

"George? Is that you, George?"

George spun around and hurried back over to the bedside of the wounded sheriff. Bryce was awake. George dropped down on his knees beside the bed, leaning in close to Bryce.

"Yeah," he said. "It's me, sheriff. It's George. Don't

worry. You're going to be all right."

"George," said Bryce, "where the hell am I?"

"You're in Mr. Hooley's house," said George. "They said they heard shots and rode out to find you beside the road. But that ain't what Charlie told us. Back in town, he said that the Hooleys had shot you. He said he seen it. He's got a posse out there right now ready to attack the house and wipe out the whole bunch."

"Stop him, George," said Bryce. "You've got to stop him. Charlie's the one who shot me."

George stared at Bryce with his mouth hanging open. Slocum had suggested that possibility, but George had not really wanted to believe it. Now there was no question, for he had just heard it from Bryce's own lips.

"Go on," said Bryce. "Hurry. Before someone gets killed out there."

"Yes, sir," said George, getting to his feet. He hurried back into the living room. "Mr. Hooley," he said, "the sheriff's awake. He said Charlie shot him. I've got to let them citizens know and stop this fight."

Jill ran toward the bedroom to see to Bryce, and Hooley stepped in front of the doorway to block George's path.

"Take it easy, George," he said.

"I got to tell them," said George.

"Of course you do," said Hooley, "but don't just go running out there. Someone might just decide to start shooting again and hit you conveniently by mistake. Now come on."

Hooley opened the door and peeked out. He could see what was left of the posse still huddled up at the far end of the lane out near the main gate, looking like a bunch of uncertain conspirators.

"It's okay," he said. "Come on."

Hooley and George walked out onto the porch together.

"Slocum," said Hooley.

Slocum stepped back up onto the porch and moved over to join Hooley and George.

"Slocum, Bryce came around, and he told George that it was Charlie who shot him."

"Just what we thought," said Slocum.

"Now, how do we let those men out there know that without someone getting shot?"

"Give me a white flag," said Slocum. "I'll walk out there with George."

"That's no guarantee," said Hooley.

"It's better than nothing," said Slocum. He looked at George. "What do you say?"

"Those are all good men out there," said George. "All except Charlie. I don't think anyone will shoot at us, you carrying a white flag."

"We got to do something, Charlie," said one of the posse men. "Either come up with some kind of plan or call the whole thing off. We can't just hang around the gate here all day."

"Damn it," said Charlie, "I'm trying to think. Give me a little time to think, will you? We're going to do something."

And he was trying to think, but nothing was coming into his head. The way he saw it, he had to make sure that Bryce was dead. Ideally, he wanted the others dead, too, even George, now that George had been in there so long. They had almost for sure told him their story, and he might just believe them.

Charlie could think of only two possibilities. One was to find a way to lead a successful attack on the ranch house, and that did not look very promising. The other was to hightail it out of the country. He decided that he would get out.

"Well, hell," he said, "I guess you're right. We ain't going to get them like this. Let's all just get mounted up and get back into town. I'll come up with some other way to handle the Hooleys and Slocum."

"What about George?" someone asked.

"Hell, I don't know," Charlie snapped back. "You all said it already. We ain't going to get to them like this. Come on. Let's get out of here."

"Wait a minute, Charlie," said one of the men. "Look."

Charlie turned back toward the house and saw George and Slocum walking side by side, coming toward the posse. Slocum was carrying a rifle with a white flag tied to the muzzle end, holding it straight up.

"Blast them," he shouted. "Blast them to hell," and he reached for his six-gun, but a man beside him grabbed his arm.

"Are you crazy, Charlie? That's George. And Slocum's carrying a white flag. Maybe he's giving himself up."

"It's some kind of trick," said Charlie. "Don't trust them."

"Charlie," said the man, still holding tight to his arm, "it's George."

Slocum and George walked on up close, and Charlie pulled himself loose from the other man's grip.

"That's Slocum," he said. "Arrest him."

"Hold on a minute," said George. "I just talked to Bryce in there."

"What?" someone said.

"He's in the house, and he ain't dead," said George. "What's more, we're all on the wrong trail out here. Bryce just told me who it was that shot him, and it wasn't Slocum, nor anyone out here at Hooley's."

Everyone turned to look at Charlie, and Charlie knew what was coming. He began backing his way through the crowd of citizens who had formed his posse, backing toward the gate and the road and the waiting horses. He was caught, and he knew it, but he wasn't about to hand them his gun and give himself up.

"It wasn't none of the Hooleys nor Slocum," said George. "It was Charlie Goober."

Charlie's revolver was out in a flash, and he snapped off a quick shot that ripped a crease in George's left shoulder. Slocum dropped his Winchester into firing position and pulled the trigger. His slug smashed Charlie's right shoulder. At almost the same time, George drew his six-gun and fired a round into Charlie's midsection. Charlie jerked and staggered. He tried to lift his revolver back up into position.

Then a member of the posse raised a gun and fired, and then another, and even when Charlie was lying dead, each member of the posse who had not yet done so stepped forward to put another bullet into the wretched, lifeless body.

"God damn," said George, "that's enough. Stop it."

"Sure," said the last man to fire a shot. "We're done, anyhow."

"Well, why don't you boys load him up and take

him on back into town with you?" George asked.

"I don't want to touch him," someone said. "He's too messy all shot up like that."

Even so, a couple of the men threw the body across the saddle of the horse Charlie had ridden, and they took it with them as they headed back toward Drownding Creek.

20

Slocum and Billy Hooley rode with George back into Drownding Creek. They intended to locate both Basil Reid and Matthew Crocker for George to arrest and put in jail on charges of murder, attempted murder, rustling, and conspiracy, just for starters.

Reid wasn't hard to find. He was with the other wounded former members of the posse in Applegate's, where several citizens had done their best to patch up the wounds. Reid had been bandaged, so George hauled him off whimpering to jail and locked him a cell.

There was no sign of Crocker. They found his store unlocked, even though the sign in the window said it was closed. They checked his house at the edge of town. He was not there. They went separate ways, agreeing to meet back at the sheriff's office. Billy was the first one to arrive back there. He stood on the sidewalk, leaning against the outside wall. A few minutes later, George returned.

"He took all his money out of the bank," George said. "Early this morning."

"Crocker?"

"Yeah," said George, "but that's all I was able to find out."

"Wonder what that means," said Billy.

"I don't know," said George. "You find out anything?"

"Nothing," said Billy. "No one's seen him today."

He looked up over George's shoulder just then and saw Slocum coming out of the livery stable next door.

"You find anything?" he called out.

"Crocker rented a horse this morning," said Slocum.

"He rented a horse," said George, "and he took all his money out of the bank. Hell, he's left town. He's on the run. Say. He probably set that posse on you all just to cover his own escape."

"Looks that way," said Slocum.

"The dirty bastard," said Billy.

"The man inside there told me that Crocker took a slow, plodding horse," said Slocum. "He ain't planning to outrun anyone on it. Where could he be going?"

There was a pause with George and Billy both thinking hard. Then George snapped his fingers.

"Railroad over at Stringtown," he said. "Let's go. We might already be too late."

• • •

Hootch Bellows was about as broke and as low as a man could get. His clothes were rags, and he had wrapped rags around his shoes to keep the soles from falling off. He hadn't had a bath or a shave in longer than he could remember, and he had forgotten what money looked like.

He was lying on the ground beside the road that ran from Drownding Creek to Stringtown, trying to sleep, hoping that sleep would make him forget for at least a little while just how hungry he was. It wasn't doing any good. He was just lying there listening to his stomach growl. Then he heard the sound of an approaching horse.

He rolled over onto his empty belly and raised his head to look through the weeds. A rider was coming. He didn't seem to be in too much of a hurry, and he had the look of a man of some means. He was wearing a gray three-piece suit and a fine looking bowler hat. He would have money, Hootch thought.

He considered walking out into the road with his hands out like a beggar and a pitiful expression on his face, but as often as not, when he did that, people just chased him away and told him to get a job. Hootch had worked a few times in his life, but he didn't like it. He didn't like having anyone telling him what to do. And he didn't like being told to go get a job. A job was an absolute last resort as far as Hootch was concerned.

He looked around and spotted there on the ground just to his right a large, nearly round rock about three times the size of his fist. He grasped it and held it and waited. The rider came closer. Hootch felt his heart pound with excitement.

Just as the rider was about to pass him by, still

clutching the rock, Hootch sprang to his feet and ran out into the road in front of the horse, waving his arms and shouting. The rider yelled. The horse whinnied and reared, and the rider toppled backward out of the saddle, landing hard enough to stun him for a moment. It was all the edge Hootch needed.

He was on top of the man in an instant, raising the rock high over his own head and bringing it down again and again, bashing the brains out of his victim. At last he stopped. He dropped the bloody rock in the road and sat there a moment, catching his breath.

Then he decided that he'd better work fast. Someone else might come along and find him there. He started going through the dead man's pockets, looking for money, and he did find a few dollars. He started to stuff the money into the pockets of his own ragged clothes, but then he thought, why waste this fine suit?

He began to strip the body. Pulling off the coat, he felt a heavy weight in one pocket. He checked it and found a revolver. He held it up and smiled broadly, then laid it aside to continue getting his new suit. He was pulling the trousers off the legs when he noticed that the horse was straying off down the road.

He abandoned the body for a moment to catch the horse, and as he was leading it back, he noticed the saddlebags. They were stuffed full. His curiosity was too much for him. The trousers would wait. He checked the bags and was astonished to find them stuffed with cash, more money than he had ever seen in his entire life. He fondled the cash for a moment, chuckling and giggling, and then he got control of himself again and looked nervously up and down the road.

He pulled the horse to the side of the road and wrapped the reins around a sapling to keep it there. He rushed back to the body and finished pulling the trousers loose. Then he got the vest and the white shirt. He picked the hat up and put it on his head, and he started to gather up the rest of the clothing, but just then three riders appeared around the bend.

"What the hell?" said George.

There in the middle of the road, the nastiest looking man he had ever seen was squatted beside the nearly naked body of another man. Even a quick glimpse was enough to show that the entire head of the dead man had been brutally bashed in.

The filthy man in the road looked up at the three riders, his mouth hanging open, his eyes wide. He was clutching in his arms what appeared to be the other's clothing. Off to the side of the road a gray mare stood grazing contentedly, oblivious to the scene of horror nearby.

"What are you doing there?" demanded George.

The man roared suddenly like a madman or a wild animal, tossed the clothing aside, and picked up a revolver from the road. He raised it and fired before any of the three could react, but his shot went wild. He thumbed the hammer back again and fired again, and Slocum drew his Colt and shot the man in the chest.

Hootch screamed as he felt the hot lead tear into his flesh and splinter his bones. He dropped the Webley and fell back, his arms wide at his sides. He thought about the suit and the gun and the horse, and he rolled his head to the side to look at the saddlebags hanging there on the gray mare. He tried to remember what all that money had looked like, and then he died.

The three riders moved forward. Slocum stopped beside the body of Hootch and looked down.

"He's dead," he said.

"I never seen anyone so ugly before in my life," said Billy.

George was looking at the other body.

"Is that Crocker?" he asked.

"It's hard to tell," said Slocum, "but that'd be my guess. It was a gray mare he rented."

George rode over to the gray mare beside the road and dismounted. He pulled open the saddlebag on the near side and reached in, coming up with a handful of bills. Then he checked the other side.

"These things are stuffed with greenbacks," he said. "Let's get these bodies out of the middle of the road and go back to town. We'll take the horse and the money. I'll send someone out with a wagon to fetch the bodies in."

He mounted up again and took hold of the gray mare's reins to lead her home.

The horse was identified by Abner Jones as the one that Crocker had rented, and a thorough search of the clothing helped establish the identity of the body beyond any reasonable doubt. The bank clerk remembered the suit as being the one that Crocker had been wearing that morning. With Crocker, Charlie, and Wade all dead, Basil Reid was the only one left alive to prosecute for the troubles at the Hooley ranch or the murder of Rolfe Wade.

Back at the ranch, Slocum and the Hooleys celebrated with a steak dinner with all the trimmings and several glasses of whiskey each, and Hooley saw to it that the entire ranch crew did as well. Bryce seemed to be doing a little better, but he was still sleeping a lot, and it would be awhile before he would eat steaks and drink whiskey, or be moved back into town. Sitting in easy chairs after the meal, Slocum and Hooley each had a glass of whiskey in their hands. Jill and Billy were still at the table.

"Slocum," said Hooley, "are you still planning to hit the trail?"

"I think I'll take off first thing in the morning," said Slocum. "I've already been around these parts for too long."

"Well," the old man said, "suit yourself, but you know, you're welcome to stick around here for as long as you like."

Slocum saw Jill give him the eye from behind her father's back.

"Thank you," he said, and he took a sip of the good brown whiskey.

"I'm sorry you lost your room," said Hooley, "but it's the only place we had to put Bryce."

"That's all right," said Slocum. "The couch will do me just fine."

And it did, too. Later, when everyone else had gone to bed, Slocum stretched out on the long couch. It was just soft enough for his comfort, a hell of a lot better than the bed up in the cabin or the cot in the jail or a blanket on the hard ground. He would sleep just fine here, he thought, covered by the one blanket.

And he was just about to drift off to sleep when he felt the touch of a soft hand on each of his cheeks. He opened his eyes to see Jill's face very close to his. And then she pressed her lips to his. Her tongue searched the inside of his mouth for a moment, and then she backed away.

"You're not too tired for this, are you?" she asked.

Slocum looked toward the stairway.

"If your daddy comes out of his room," he said, "he can look straight down here on this couch."

Jill stood up and smiled down at Slocum. She was wearing a long robe, and she started to unfasten its ties. She pulled it open in front, and he could see that she had nothing on beneath it. He looked at her round, firm breasts and then down at the dark triangle at her crotch. She slipped the robe off her shoulders and let it drop to the floor.

"He'll be sleeping like a log up there all night long," she said, and she crawled under the blanket to stretch out her naked body on top of his.

"Hell," said Slocum. "Maybe I will stick around for just a few more days."

If you enjoyed this book, subscribe now and get...

TWO FREE

A $7.00 VALUE—

If you would like to read more of the very best, most exciting, adventurous, action-packed Westerns being published today, you'll want to subscribe to True Value's Western Home Subscription Service.

Each month the editors of True Value will select the 6 very best Westerns from America's leading publishers for special readers like you. You'll be able to preview these new titles as soon as they are published, *FREE* for ten days with no obligation!

TWO FREE BOOKS

When you subscribe, we'll send you your first month's shipment of the newest and best 6 Westerns for you to preview. With your first shipment, two of these books will be yours as our introductory gift to you absolutely *FREE* (a $7.00 value), regardless of what you decide to do. If you like them, as much as we think you will, keep all six books but pay for just 4 at the low subscriber rate of just $2.75 each. If you decide to return them, keep 2 of the titles as our gift. No obligation.

Special Subscriber Savings

When you become a True Value subscriber you'll save money several ways. First, all regular monthly selections will be billed at the low subscriber price of just $2.75 each. That's at least a savings of $4.50 each month below the publishers price. Second, there is never any shipping, handling or other hidden charges—*Free home delivery*. What's more there is no minimum number of books you must buy, you may return any selection for full credit and you can cancel your subscription at any time. A TRUE VALUE!